Samantha Trayhurn is currently undertaking a Doctor of Creative Arts under the supervision of Anthony Uhlmann, Ben Etherington and Gail Jones. Samantha is interested in world literature as a process for exploring non-unitary, post-human subjectivity. She is influenced by Spinoza's monism, as well as theorists such as Gilles Deleuze & Felix Guattari, and Rosi Braidotti.

Samantha has a Bachelor of Arts (Hons) from Griffith University, and a Bachelor of Science. She is interested in expanding upon a cross-disciplinary creative arts practice that investigates global ecologies, both natural and conceptual. Her PhD novel is concerned with exploring transcultural topologies through migration, interspecies subjectivity and transcorporeality.

Samantha has had creative work published in *LiNQ* Journal, *Pure Slush* and *Art Ascent*. In 2017, she presented at the Australasian Association for Literatures 'Literary Environments: Place, Planet and Translation' conference, and organises live readings and creative workshops via CrossCurrent Creative. Her social commentary also appears in the *Overland* online magazine.

I0562779

Interactive Press
Brisbane

My Father is a Curlew

Samantha Trayhurn

Glass House Books
an imprint of IP (Interactive Publications Pty Ltd)
Treetop Studio • 9 Kuhler Court
Carindale, Queensland, Australia 4152
sales@ipoz.biz
http://ipoz.biz/shop
First published by IP in 2025
© 2025 Samantha Trayhurn (text); IP (design)

Printed in 14 pt Avenir Book on Caslon Pro 12 pt.

ISBN: 9781923435100 (PB) 9781923435117 (eBook)

A catalogue record for this book is available from the National Library of Australia

NATIONAL
LIBRARY
OF AUSTRALIA

To the curlew that came to me and delivered this book—
may your ancestors circle this earth forever.

Contents

Prologue

It is inevitable: flowers in a vase always remind me of mortality, so naturally, standing in the Art Gallery of New South Wales, I think of my father. Before a large gilt frame, I take a deep breath. Painted insects nestle between soft pink petals. To the left, an unopened bulb guides my eye towards a butterfly perched on a red chrysanthemum. I exhale and can't be sure if the tears burning my cheeks are for my father, or if they come from an intense appreciation of the painting's vivid depth.

Then, I notice it. A reflection in the vase: an upside-down image of a window sliced into segments by panels, and, beyond the room that contains the window, a sky etched with grey clouds. A flock of birds passes by the painted window. I blink to focus – to be sure of what I am seeing. My father glides among the birds, narrow shoulders stretching and contracting, arms beating like wings. He is smiling.

For a suspended moment, I feel like I am looking down at myself, watching from the vantage of my father as he flies from the frame and circles the ceiling of the gallery. The motion makes me dizzy, but I assign it to a lingering jetlag: the sensation of still not feeling entirely present in any one place. In the week since I returned from my trip through Europe, ever since the phone call from Oji on the way home from the airport, there has been a peripheral chatter scoring my days.

Wiping my eyes, I look away from the image and slide back into my skin. The guard in the corner gives me a sympathetic smile. I wonder if he observes such displays of emotion every day. I want to ask how often beauty moves people to tears, or, how often they mask real sorrow behind appreciation, but I don't. Ultimately, I feel that, like a psychologist's interior knowledge of her patients, the information shouldn't be shared beyond the invisible cubicle enclosing the viewer, the guard, and the painting.

If asked to measure the minutes in worldly terms rather than the expanses that exist within a compartment containing my body and a still-life, I couldn't say how long I had been standing staring at the painted reflection of the window in the vase, but, when I finally shift my weight and look at my watch, I realise that the gallery will soon be closing.

1

My father is a bird. My father is an island. My father is a box of matches. My father is a chewed pen. My father is a silver coin. My father is the lint at the bottom of my handbag. My father is the colour the water turns when the light drains out. My father is a brown mirror.

Over the deck of the ferry, a flock of curlews obstruct the sky with outstretched wings. Their bodies are sinewy and gaunt. I wonder how recently they arrived from their long southern migration. How tired their bodies are. My father dedicated his life to the study of migratory birds, but I can't understand why. Flying all the way to your breeding grounds in Siberia just to find your food source has hatched early and has already been depleted or plummeting from the sky like a torpedo from the hull of a plane, seems like a flaw in the evolutionary system. Surely, there must be a more economical way.

I remember my father flying among the birds in the painting, and I look for him above the boat, but I'm not sure what his defining avian characteristics might be. Whether human traits carry on between forms. A tangle of flight paths threads over and under as the last sunlight radiates through the loosely knitted clouds. I feel the tang of brine on my face and the cool flow of dusk into my body. It is six in the evening. Behind the boat, ripples rise from the engine and extend over Redland Bay. It's not like the bays around Sydney that are fringed with expensive houses and speckled with small, sandy beaches. The water undulating against the ferry is brown and turbid and along the shore, laps against mudflats. A man with matted shoulder length hair, a neon green t-shirt and Hawaiian board shorts, looks me up and down while taking a long swig from his litre bottle of iced coffee. I guess that he is going home rather than visiting. There are islands in his eyes.

The vessel is full of locals laden with bags, returning from their business on the mainland. I sit in the outdoor section at the back of the boat, wedged between a metal railing and a gruff elderly woman. Her leathery skin reminds me of pressing against Grandma Sue on the bench seat of the old HR Holden that struggled to make it up the winding seaside hills on the way to school. I miss Grandma Sue. I miss her laugh, like a Kookaburra warming up, and the way she unleashed it generously. She surfed until she was fifty-five. Never wore a bra. She took me on hikes in the Blue Mountains, and we shouted our wishes into the vast crevasses of ancient rock. Merry, merry king of the bush was she. She was the closest thing to a father I ever had.

I think about the last time I saw my father; the only time I saw him since I was a baby. We met briefly before my trip to Europe, and he wore the clothes one might expect of a university scientist: high-waisted khakis and a short-sleeved button up shirt tucked into a cheap synthetic belt. He had an oily complexion pocked with visible pores and wiry hairs protruding from his face. He was in Sydney for a conference, and I had nervously dialed the number that Jill received from a friend when word circulated that Aki Matsumoto was back in the city. I pictured that it would be like a movie where an adult child comes to know her ageing, estranged parent and, rather than the obligatory love that evolves over a lifetime, they build a friendship based on a mutual like for each other. It wasn't like that, though. When I walked into the sleek Glebe café, he was already sitting by the window. He had an expression of bored resignation, usually reserved for doctor's waiting rooms. He stood up and greeted me with a handshake.

Apart from a few text messages and failed attempts to arrange another meeting, we hadn't spoken again. Deep down, I thought it was only a matter of time until we started to bridge the gulf that had opened over a lifetime apart. It's what I wanted. Then, the phone call with Oji settled the matter once and for all. I would never get to know my father.

'I tried to phone you, Wallace,' he muttered, 'but there was no way to reach you. Then I spoke to your mother, and she said it was best to wait, not to spoil your trip. There was an accident. I'm sorry.'

The small ferry pulls into the first stop at Karragarra Island. I inhale the aromatic blend of eucalypts and acacias that fringe the coastline. Flattened and elongated, the small landmass juts from the surface of the water like a half-submerged dugong. Evening shimmers with humidity as the sky transitions from rose to lilac.

The first stars appear.

Cramped and uncomfortable on the hard bench, I sweat through my cotton t-shirt. Moisture slickens the join of skin between the woman and me. When she adjusts her position, she spreads her legs a little wider, leaning forward, asserting that I am a guest in her space. Her movements are in stark contrast to the small Japanese woman who sat next to me on the plane ride from Sydney to Brisbane and had space to rest her handbag between her body and the armrest, but still politely leaned away.

The first thing I noticed upon boarding the flight was that about half of the passengers were Japanese. The budget carrier connected Sydney from Tokyo, before continuing its journey to Brisbane. The airhostess strode down the aisle pushing a cart, her heavy makeup cracking under the hard lights. When she arrived at our row, she nodded at the old woman and me as if we were travelling together and asked us a question. I didn't understand, but rather than fumble my way through an apology about how I don't speak the language, I smiled and pointed at the red wine.

I remembered all the times in school that my classmates asked me to say something in Japanese: greetings, swear words, the names of food. I spat out strange sounds, and no one ever knew the difference.

As the boat idles, I angle my body away again, crossing my legs and pressing my shoulder into the rail. The woman next to me coughs a phlegmy smoker's cough without covering her mouth. Spittle lands on the back of my hand.

'Karragarra,' she says. 'Karragarra Island.'

The boat lowers its plank and a family disembarks. I watch the young couple – mother cradling a baby, and father pulling a boy of about six by the hand. They walk down the jetty to a solitary 4WD parked in the bays by the boat ramp. I wonder how long would it take to walk the perimeter of the island with those small legs? What would it be like to grow up in such a place?

An alternative story flickers through my mind like a racing shoal of fish just below the surface of the water. I construct a version of events in which my father didn't leave my mother and me. One in which we didn't move south to live with my grandmother until she died ten years ago. One in which we didn't sell the Maroubra apartment for significantly more than it was purchased for in the 70s, acquiring a tidy inheritance that gave me luxuries that most women my age don't have.

On the boxy television mounted to a beam running along the roof of the boat, advertisements for local businesses scroll over and over. *Curlew Homes, Curlew Early Learning Centre...* I begin to understand why my father chose to settle in this place. Whenever Jill talked about their fieldwork tracking bird migrations in the nineties, she always looked up, as though the man she had once known had also flown away.

At ten years old, I read everything I could find on migration in the textbooks that lined Jill's overflowing bookshelf. I marveled at the old British naturalists like Charles Morton who, unable to understand where all the birds went from season to season, conjured their own versions. In some accounts, they flew to the moon, in others, they hibernated under the mudflats of ponds. I explained to my best friend Sarah that the birds' paths must be circulatory, and, by that logic, my father should too one day return. When he never did I often thought of him, year after year, passing through a constellation of coordinates within the unbounded dome of sky, looking down, but not stopping.

Sarah.

I try to think of the wise, calm words she would offer if she knew how nervous I was right now, but all I can see are her disappointed eyes when I left her apartment last week.

Nearing Russell Island, I watch as a large curlew cuts towards the wetlands, its streaked wings expanding effortlessly, while its horizontal body glides towards the ground, extending a landing gear of spindly legs. It digs its talons into the mud where tubular bristles sprout from the banks like rotting fingers.

Passengers begin to disembark.

'Thanks, Joe,' a middle-aged woman in a floral mumu shouts to the driver sitting with the cabin door open, top button undone, an earring in one ear.

'Catch you next time, Louise,' he waves.

I wait for the crowd to clear, surveying the island's perimeter for signs of what my days here might hold. To the north strong tides claw at the rocks. Beyond the mudflats, fat grey stones pocked with oyster shells dapple the bank. It is far removed from the tropical islands on the billboards in the Brisbane airport.

I don't want half of a house on some backwater hunk of land in the middle of Redland Bay, but I can't help wondering why my father left it to me and what else I might find here. I wait as everyone shuffles off the boat. I try not to be judgmental, but most of them have shabby clothes and unkempt hair. A few aren't wearing shoes.

When the boat empties of its final passengers, I sigh and realise that I am really doing this. I pull my backpack from the luggage rack and cart it down the covered walkway towards the meeting area. On the outward facing wall of the neighbouring walkway, a tiled mosaic sparkles. Rainbow shards piece together an impressive aquatic scene. Sky blending to water. An eagle soars over scrub, while a dugong scours the sea grass. The letters for 'Russell Island' contain small sunsets – yellow fading to orange fading to red – and wedged disproportionately to the very left, the letters of the Indigenous name, 'Canaipa,' press almost against the 'R', as though added as an afterthought.

Reaching the end of the jetty, I scan the small crowd of faces for the man I spoke to on the phone.

'I'm confused; how did you say you knew my father?' I asked him.

Oji's voice chimed. 'Oh, I apologise. Your father and I knew each other for a very long time. My name is Makoto Oji, but it's a bit of a mouthful I know! Please, just call me Oji. It's easier, and it means Uncle in Japanese. I think Aki would have liked that.'

I felt a quick surge of anger at reference to the desires of my father, a man who had shown so little interest in what I wanted, but it quickly passed when I felt the sting of the past tense. I spent a long time as a teenager being angry with my father, but the anger faded as I got older, and eventually I just wanted to know him. To know where I came from.

My stomach churns as I spot Oji easily among the handful of people standing next to the jetty. His bald head shines; his white linen suit is crisp against his olive skin. I lift my hand in greeting, and, meeting my eye, he waves back enthusiastically. I take a deep breath and step off the jetty onto solid land.

The bird on the shore tilts its head back and lets out a loud, sad *currrlllleeeeeeeee.*

The room is small and square.

'I apologise it is so small,' Oji says, depositing me in the doorway with my bags.

The new moonlight casts a gauzy shadow across peeling paint.

'No, it's great,' I lie.

Dust floats in the air. The space smells doggy and mildewed, but I don't think Oji has any pets. He bows his head with that same humility I saw during the meeting with my father. The fragrant potpourri hanging in a bag on the doorknob doesn't quite mask the dankness. A single bed is pressed against the back wall, slumping in the middle of the mattress – there is a wooden nightstand ringed with cup marks – three uneven stacks of old books – a dozen taped up cardboard boxes – an antique wooden chair in the corner with a broken leg.

'Don't sit there,' Oji warns.

Suppressing a yawn, I long to curl against the hard springs, adding my own contours. I haven't been sleeping well. It's like when I spent hours staring at the surf from Grandma Sue's balcony and later, when I closed my eyes, I felt like I was on a boat – a slight rocking – the blackness forming into peaks. Now, the canvas behind my closed eyes is contoured with slow moving wing beats. White at the edges.

'Do you need anything?' Oji asks.

I shake my head.

Oji bows again and I note how the incline of his head has a geniality that my father didn't display, at least not on the occasion of our meeting. Aware of the risk of assigning sentiments actually intended for my father to this man, I focus on the kindness emanating from Oji. A small and round face with a creased brow, lips resting in a soft smile.

'Thanks for having me stay. I know this must be a bit hard.'

'Not at all.'

He nods his head this time, much quicker and sharper than the bow. Then, not wanting to intrude on a woman's first moments in an unfamiliar space in case he should witness some secret ritual, he averts his eyes, turns, and walks back down the narrow laminate hallway to the kitchen.

Even though I have only spoken to him twice before meeting him today, I gather that this is the kind of man Oji is: one with traditional values and a knack for quiet, well-timed courtesy. I encountered men like that in my travels; solitary souls that read both sides of the safety instruction card on airplanes and looked up attentively as the hostess pointed the way to the nearest exits without the slightest hint of hurry or annoyance.

I drag my bag over the carpet stains that mirror the watermarks on the roof and close the door.

Flopping down onto the creaking bed, I sigh as my phone rings in my pocket again. I turn the volume down, glance at the notifications on the screen, then turn it over onto the mattress.

Missed call Jill.

Missed call Sarah.

Missed call Unknown.

Stretching my legs out so that my toes touch the bottom of the bed, I close my eyes. I know I should call Jill, I know I should call Sarah, and I know I should call the lawyers about the paperwork for the house, but I don't want to think about any of those things right now.

There is a knock at the door, gentle like a branch rubbing against an awning.

Oji's gentle voice prompts from outside. 'Would you like to eat?'

'Yes, yes, thank you. I'll be right there.'

I lift myself from the sunken mattress and leave my phone on the bedside table, the message notification glaring like a beacon in the right-hand corner of the screen.

In the dining room – a nook off the half-renovated kitchen – the table is set for two.

A bottle of uncorked imported red wine, a leafy green salad in a bamboo dish, a plate piled with skewers of vegetables and fried tofu. At the smell of food, I am ravenous.

'It looks great.'

Oji appears from the kitchen carrying a ceramic bowl filled with soba noodles.

'Sit, please sit!'

He places the bowl down and pours two glasses of pinot noir. I pull out a chair and arrange myself at the stained pine table. There are no placemats, just two settings consisting of brassy cutlery and chipped plates. It is a stark contrast to Jill's apartment with every item sourced from glossy catalogues or high-end antique stores. I take in the scene of how my father would have spent his evenings, wondering what he and Oji would have talked about.

I scan the living room. The mismatched furniture reminds me of a share house I lived in briefly last year when I had a fight with my mother and tried to prove my independence. Everything is functional, but without a hint of design. Among the plastic sheets and paint cans lining the floor, there are four different shades of wood.

Oji sits opposite me at the table, so we are obliged to make eye contact.

'I hope the bedroom is okay.'

I smile awkwardly, ladling food onto my plate. 'Yes, it's good. Thank you again.'

Now that I am alone in this house with an old man I don't know, I realise just how strange my decision to come really was. I didn't think about the particulars at all – like how many meals we would share, or how many conversations we would need to have. I have so many questions that I want to ask, but I don't know how to broach them, so I focus on the food.

'What is this? It smells incredible.'

Oji smiles. 'Just some vegetable yakitori. Nothing special.'

The only Japanese food I have ever eaten is from the restaurants in the city. The plates usually come in elegant small portions with flowers on the side, or ornate garnishes of pickled ginger. This spread is large and homely. I pull a seared mushroom off the skewer with my teeth.

'Do you cook?' Oji asks.

I laugh. In our house, after Grandma Sue passed away, it was mostly take-away and dinner at friends' houses while Jill worked late.

'Well, maybe we can do something about that while you're here,' Oji says. 'Your father was a great cook.'

My smile falters. I am in my father's house, at my father's table for the first time in my life, and he isn't here. My thoughts return to the first phone conversation with Oji – an accident he said, but didn't give any details. I was so shocked and tired that I didn't ask for any, and now that I am here Oji seems too fragile to press. There are already cracks in his pleasant expressions – sadness showing through – and I feel like if I say the wrong thing he will break open entirely. I'm not ready for that.

'An accident?' Jill raised her eyebrows, as though she didn't believe it, but she promised that she didn't know any more than I did. 'You'll have to ask Oji when you get there.'

There was bitterness in her voice. My mother wasn't happy that I had decided to go to the island. I could tell that she was annoyed about this new forced connection to my father that the house presented. Now, I wonder if I am sitting in my father's chair, or if his was the empty one at the head. I glance at the vacant space and Oji quickly changes the subject.

'So, tell me about Spain. That's where you were for the last part of your trip yes? I have always wanted to see the Park Guell.'

My attention shifts, and I smile at the reference to Antonio Gaudi. 'It's wonderful. Everyone is so concerned with the Sagrada Familia, but the Park was the real highlight,' I reminisce, retracing the undulating walkways, reveling in the absence of angles.

I am standing before the mosaic dragon, the pads of its tiled talons wrapping around the balustrades of a wide staircase. I look up to the sloping archway, fringed with yellow chrysanthemums, threaded along a splintered green backdrop of broken tiles. I lead Oji towards the central courtyard with my words. He listens, nodding in delight.

Once I relax, I find it particularly easy to converse with Oji. He is unlike any man I have ever met. With men my age, and even my university professors, I am always lost for words. I become a sounding board as they charge onwards, eagerly filling the silences that I leave. Oji is different. He waits patiently for his turn to speak, encourages me to go on when I hit a topic that interests me, and, best of all, doesn't pry too deeply about what I am going to do now that I have finished my degree.

After some time, I notice that I have been doing most of the talking and I still know almost nothing about the man sitting across from me.

'What do you do?'

'Oh, nothing much. Crosswords, mostly.'

'Have you travelled a lot?'

'A little, here and there. To the grocery store and back at least twice a week.'

Oji skillfully steers the conversation towards peripheral subjects, offering tidbits of island trivia. The RSL club occasionally has live music on the weekends. The best place to watch the sunrise is just around the bend at Sandy Beach. Laura Coy studied art too, and paints fabulous mandalas. Yes, despite the beliefs of most city-folk, it is possible to buy a decent cup of coffee here. Kate at the café by the jetty makes the best.

Time flows around us effortlessly as a tide.

'Can I ask why he left it to me?' I probe once the wine has given me some confidence. 'His share in the property, I mean.'

Oji pauses for a moment, stops eating, rests his elbows on the table and brings his hands together in front of his chest. 'To be honest, I don't know. He didn't talk that much about you. You and your mother represented a different time in Aki's life, long before me, so I never pushed him too hard for information. I knew he met with you, we spoke a little about that, but that was all.'

'And do you know why he never arranged to see me again after we met?'

'No. You have to understand your father was a very private man. When the doctors said he didn't have long, all I can imagine is that he didn't want to burden you with his illness. It was very like him.'

A gecko scurries across the kitchen wall and clicks loudly. Oji follows it with his eyes.

'What do you mean he didn't have long?'

'Oh, I assumed you knew… lung cancer… it was progressing very quickly. I thought he told you when you met. He wanted to, I think.'

I think back to the meeting with my father, but I had no reference point to measure his health against. He seemed old, tired even, but that might have been his usual state. He didn't speak about being sick, or much of anything. Did his illness have something to do with the accident? Before I can ask, Oji continues.

'It makes sense in a way. I think being sick was why…' Oji chooses his words carefully, 'why he didn't want to become too involved with you. He was very surprised when you called and probably didn't want to start a relationship when he knew he had so little time. For both of your sakes. Knowing your father, he probably thought telling you would be unkind, especially if he knew you were about to go on a big life-defining trip. He probably thought he had no right to your sympathy after all these years. Perhaps the house was his way of saying…'

He doesn't finish. There are certain things that apologies can't mend. I let Oji's words sink in and they sink quickly like an anchor.

'Are you mad?' I ask. 'That he didn't consult you about giving half of the house to me?'

Oji shakes his head vigorously. 'No. Half of this house, this land, was his. He was welcome to do with it as he pleased. We knew each other a long time. When he found out he was sick about a year ago, we decided to move here from Okinawa. He always spoke so fondly of this part of the world, and it seemed a better place for him to be. We came to live here together, but there was no agreement that he would leave everything to me. We were still very independent, in our own ways.'

'Did you want it, though?'

Oji squeezes his eyes closed for a moment and then opens them as though looking at the question anew.

'I don't want to leave, if that's what you mean,' I say. 'I guess that's something we can talk about while you're here.'

'Don't worry, I'm not going to try and kick you out or anything.'

Oji bows his head deeply then takes a long sip from his glass.

'Thank you. Well, in the meantime while you decide what you want to do, you are welcome to stay for as long as you like. Goodness knows, I could use the help with the renovations.'

I glance around at the plates and utensils stacked precariously on the laminate bench tops, the cabinets removed. Oji catches me grimacing at the cracked green linoleum. It really is putrid.

'That has to go next,' he laughs.

'It's not that bad,' I lie.

We sit with the insincerity for a moment and then both laugh louder.

'The wine is very good, yes?'

I nod in agreement feeling as airy as the lace curtains. My thoughts slip through the perforations. I let them go.

2

Fish flesh holds the light in.

I sit on the bench at the end of the jetty and watch two boys cast fishing lines over the edge. Close together in age, they have their hair cut in shaggy mops. One's is cropped short with a rat's tail extending down his back, the other's is trimmed around his ears falling into a long mullet. A little girl in baggy pink knickers, and nothing else, circles, begging for a turn.

'Piss off, Milly,' one of the boys hisses, 'fishing isn't for girls. Go put some clothes on!'

She crosses her arms over her chest to cover her coin-flat nipples, and with a huff, kicks the bucket over, crying her way all the way down the jetty.

The bucket spills a haul of tiny bream over the concrete. The silvery forms twist against the hard ground, gasping for air. The light seems to move inside them as they writhe, as though pearlescent blood is circulating under the surface of the skin. Along the beach of Russell Island there are a few jetties like this one, where boats can moor, or people can throw a line. Being in a place that is only accessible by boat is an unusual feeling. A heady stillness in the air makes it feel like I am inside a snow-globe and the rest of the world has faded away. I have the strange thought that at any moment someone could pick up the globe and shake it and the whole bay would rise and envelop me.

I hold the phone closer to my ear. Jill is talking about a reality show where total strangers get married to each other.

'Sorry, it's a bit noisy here.'

'Where are you? It sounds like a daycare centre.'

'Just down by the jetty. What were you saying?'

The boy with the mullet grasps his rod tightly.

'So, anyway. The guy ended up being a real spiritual type. Meditation, candles, crystals, the whole lot. And she was a lawyer. The look on her face when he took her hand and started chanting a mantra at the reception. It was hilarious. He was good looking, though.'

'You know those shows are marketed towards bored housewives and desperate singles. You need to get a hobby.'

Sometimes, I find it hard to believe that my mother has a doctorate in biology.

'Oh, don't be such a snob. It's entertaining. Plus, I'm thinking about applying.'

'You can't be serious?'

'Why not? They pay for everything. I'd at least get a nice ring. And I'm certainly not meeting anyone at the office. All the men are married, or gay... yes, I can spot that a little better now... or half my age. Not that I'm against that. But there's all the HR drama I'd have to deal with. Not after what happened to Katrina last year. Have you ever heard of a woman being sued for sexual harassment? No, thank you.'

'Of course women can be sued for sexual harassment.'

'I was thinking about applying for the one with the farmers, too, to better my odds, but, if I'm really honest, I couldn't be a farmer's wife. I've grown too accustomed to good city coffee. And all that laundry I'd have to do!'

I laugh at the thought of my mother dressed in a frilly wedding dress on national television. The worst part is, I can imagine it.

The nose of the boy's rod dips down as he reels with all his strength. Another bream no more than ten centimetres in length bobs on the end of the line. He cheers loud enough for Jill to hear.

'What are you doing there anyway?'

I haven't been here long, but time seems stretched out like my distance from the mainland. Each day is painted in water colours that blend and merge.

'Oh, you know. This and that. Just taking a break at the moment. I've been helping with the house renovations, actually.'

'House renovations! Wallace, what about applying for jobs? What happened with that internship?'

I sigh. 'Not now.'

'Then when? You need to think about these things.'

'I know!'

I hear the shrillness of my own voice and feel instantly guilty. I hate snapping at my mother.

Just as I was trying to decide whether or not to visit the island, I received a phone call from a boutique counter-culture gallery in Surry Hills. The woman announced herself, slowly enunciating every syllable.

'Ursula Karlsson, we met on Wednesday.'

I remembered her: platinum blonde hair, tall, dressed in a charcoal pantsuit. I'd handed in my CV to appease my mother, but the truth is, I hate the kind of work that Ursula displays in her gallery. I am drawn to big, old paintings that make all those pop-art hangovers seem insignificant. I can't imagine three hundred years from now, anyone crossing continents to see anything that Ursula deems worthy of her walls. While I was in Europe with all those Vermeers and Breughels and Van Eycks, I felt there was something profound about standing before the immensity of a moment blown up and made static for hundreds of years.

Ursula told me that, in fact, she was looking for a curatorial intern and was impressed by my application, which was nothing more than a single page outlining the exhibition I put on for my graduate project, and my very average GPA.

I made up my mind. Clearing my throat, I told Ursula that, while I would usually be honoured, I sadly had to decline.

'A family emergency,' I sighed, 'I'll be leaving right away.'

Disconnecting the call, I wondered what clothes I should pack for a Queensland Spring.

My mother's voice again. 'Wallace, You're in this strange place all by yourself. I'm worried about you. When are you coming back?'

I can't help noticing that Jill was much less concerned about my whereabouts when I was on the other side of the world for two months. I know that me being here, in my father's dwelling place, is upsetting her.

'I'm not all by myself. Oji's here. And I don't know when I'm coming back yet.'

The other boy has taken the fish from his friend and is now driving his own hook back into its cheek. I watch on in disbelief.

'Oji. Tell me about this Oji. Do you know anything about what happened yet?'

The fish slowly goes limp on the line.

'No, Oji is quiet. But nice. Simple. I haven't asked. I don't know if he wants to talk about it.'

'Then what do you hope to achieve? By being there?'

The boy tosses the rod back over his shoulder with the fish attached and flings it out into the bay in the hopes of landing a bigger catch. The line propels into the air, and the fish comes loose, gliding weightlessly for a moment before landing in the water with a heavy plop.

'Good one, idiot!' The mullet boy yells in frustration.

The city, with its suits and trains and lunch specials in plastic containers, seems very far away. The dry eucalypts rustle overhead as a strong southerly wind starts to blow, filling the air with a dense fragrance. The towering trees drop fresh foliage and gumnuts. I notice a thick matt of vegetation building up in the carpark. I can't imagine there are street sweepers here like there are back home, coming around before dawn to erase the disorder of days passing. I want to tell my mother that I don't really hope to achieve anything; I'd just like to stay a while longer and get to know this place. It isn't big – a main bitumen road runs down from the jetty to the rear side of the island and is intersected by a few more paved roads, and many more dirt ones. A lot of houses are still being built, and there are empty lots pressed up against bushland ready for new inhabitants. I've driven up and and down the streets with Oji, but I haven't quite figured out what to make of the place yet – I don't know if it excites or unsettles me. Probably a mixture of both.

'Wallace, I just don't understand. Come home and we can get the lawyers to manage anything else that needs to be done.'

'I know. I just… I don't know. Look, I've got to go, but I'll call you in a couple of days, ok?'

'Ok. But at least watch the show tonight. I think they've got an Italian bus driver marrying a single mum, and he's going to sing to her at the altar. Looks romantic.'

'If you say so.' I hang up.

I wonder if Jill and my father were ever romantic. I suppose they must have been at one stage, but I don't know anything about their story. Jill never wanted to talk about it. And I never saw her with another man. She always said she was too busy, but I wonder if he broke her heart. Or if she invested all the love she had into me after he left.

Watching the bay, I take the only photo of my father that I have out of my wallet. I found the Polaroid while going through Jill's storage unit and folded it behind my bankcards. I was looking for some remnant of him, and it was all there was. The scene is not so different from the one that stretches before me. Jill must have taken the photo in that brief moment when we were a family.

In the image, it was an overcast day by the Moreton Bay foreshore. Baby Wallace twisted her body as her father attempted to cradle her. One leg hung between his forearm and his chest while her tiny left hand reached for his chin. At the precise moment the shutter was pressed, he was looking down at her smiling, and her face was screwed up about to unleash a tirade of tears.

While I was too young to remember the day, I have padded the snapshot with a whole made-up series of events. Strong arms sailed my body down in a swooping arc so that my feet skimmed the water, I unleashed shrieks of joy; there was a picnic lunch with peanut butter sandwiches that made me smack my chubby cheeks with uncertainty at the way my tongue stuck to the inside of my mouth.

I look up as mullet boy gives another whoop of glee. He has landed a bigger catch. The rod nearly breaks in two as he reels it in, his friend holding him around the waist for support.

I walk back down the jetty and, nearing the car park, see the little girl sitting on a bench in the waiting bay. She is hugging her knees to her chest; a shining stream of mucus runs down her chin. She sees me and pushes her russet hair from her eyes.

'Hey.' I stop beside her. 'You're Milly, aren't you?'

She doesn't answer, just takes a deep breath to swallow her tears.

'I'm Wallace,' I continue. 'I like your...'

I've spoken to enough children to know that a sure way to get them to open up is to pay them a compliment – on their clothes, their toys – but this little girl, almost naked, is just skin, bones and cheap synthetic underwear. I stumble for a word.

'Hair,' I decide. 'I like your hair. I always wanted red hair.'

'Max says it's ugly,' she whispers.

'Is Max your brother?'

Milly nods.

'Well, brothers don't know what they're talking about if you ask me. What do boys know about hair? Plus, I saw his hair, and it wasn't that flash.'

At this, Milly laughs. Her thin lips open wide to reveal uneven teeth, the new ones bearing deep grooves, a large gap next to her canine.

'Max is ugly!' she shrieks.

'Shhhh, I didn't say that.'

I look over my shoulder to where the boys continue to fish. The tide is going out and the jetty stands over dark grey mud. The pillars are covered in empty oyster shells. The breeze continues to pick up, and a pungent fishy aroma mixes with the eucalyptus.

Milly lowers her knees, revealing bare white skin, bruised at the waist. 'Do you have any friends?'

'Not here. Not really. I had a friend where I used to live.'

'I don't have any friends, either,' Milly confides, lowering her eyes. 'I don't go to school.'

I try to gauge how old she is, and I guess at six or seven, but she speaks with a voice much younger.

'Would you like to be my friend?'

Her eyes light up and she nods. She springs to her feet and grabs my hand.

'We can be best friends!'

'Oi, Milly!' Max has spotted us. 'I told you to go home!'

'I'm talking to my friend!'

'Now! Or I'll tell Dad you've been a little bitch again.'

Milly's eyes darken and fresh tears start to flow. She drops my hand and takes three bounding barefooted steps across the bitumen.

'I hate you!'

'It's okay,' I try to soothe her, but her eyes have gone blank.

She lifts her small, grimy hand and waves as she runs towards home.

The island is never quiet, but in a different way to how the city is never quiet. Where the traffic hummed, the air crackles with insects. Crowded streets filled with chatter and the clack of heels are replaced by a cacophony of lorrikeets. The days pass like dreams; slow when they are taking place but fading quickly into each other so that it becomes difficult to discern between them.

Two weeks in, Spring gives way to Summer early, and the heat is stifling. It feels like you could grab at the air and come away with a fistful of it. I don't remember Summer like this, but maybe that's because my city life was so often lived in a quick commute between air-conditioned buildings. The air-conditioner at Oji's doesn't work. Even so, it is satisfying helping him with the renovations. I like the way my muscles ache and the way that sweat pools in the grooves of my collarbones. We don't talk much as we work, usually dividing the tasks over different areas of the house, except when a particular job requires two, and we come together, finding a steady pace, watching the other's body for an indication of which point needs extra elevation or a strong push.

Over dinner, we share brief reports of the day and recount snippets of news from the radio that drifts unevenly from its perch on a chair under the cracked patio. The politicians are still arguing about the marriage plebiscite; there's another biker gang crime syndicate on the Gold Coast; a celebrity couple is in trouble for smuggling their pets into the country on a private jet.

'We are getting low on white paint.'

'I'll get some more tomorrow. Some nails too.'

'Did you hear the latest on North Korea?'

The pile of debris grows larger and larger. The damp plywood from the old kitchen cabinets and carpet from the living room, now ripped out, settles into the dirt and creates an earthy odour that wafts into the kitchen at mealtimes. The bare concrete floor is cold underfoot.

In the yard, weeds and vines cover the entire perimeter of the fence, clasping the pile on all sides, appearing to hold everything in place.

I wipe sweat from my forehead as the afternoon sun bears down. The Queensland sun is different, more determined. While

I work, I uncover a village of snails hiding under some cracked pavers and feel an affinity with the small nomads carrying their homes on their backs.

If Oji is concerned about how long I will be staying, he shows no signs. He has started asking for my input: what colour paint would I like in the bedrooms? What kind of flooring would look best in the living areas?

'Technically, we're partners now,' he reminded me last night as we pawed over brochures like children doing a school project. My phone vibrated on the coffee table, but I ignored it.

Missed call Jill

Missed call Sarah

Missed call Unknown

I stack the last of the old pavers to the side and look across the garden to where Oji is pulling large weeds from what might become a garden bed but is currently a bald patch among thick growth that blends all the way back to the bush. With his shirt tied around his head to catch the sweat, he doesn't necessarily look younger, but more dexterous.

When we leave the house, we usually just go as far as the IGA to stock up on supplies. The fruit and vegetable section is sad and scarce. Most of the time, the large wooden bins are nearly empty, the hessian coverings at the bottom exposed, the produce on the verge of turning. Soft and over-ripe tomatoes. Bananas pocked with black bruises, fruit flies circling. Potatoes with green and yellow nubs sprouting like young, bare trees.

'If you want things really fresh, you've got to go to the mainland,' Oji tells me. 'Or a lot of people grow their own.'

He picks a bag of carrots that still look crisp from the refrigerated section. 'Get whatever you like.'

I put a few items into the trolley: a bag of spinach, the best bananas I can find, a punnet of mushrooms.

We make our way up and down the aisles, Oji crossing off a list.

'I like to try and get everything in one trip so I don't have to come back. I'm a bit of a hermit these days.'

I laugh. 'Me, too, you could say. I've barely spoken to anyone since I arrived. I feel like I'm in hiding.'

'But, the important question is, what are you hiding from?'

'Very Mr. Miyagi of you,' I grin, ignoring the question.

He looks at me wide-eyed, and I know that he doesn't understand the reference.

'You've never seen *The Karate Kid*?'

'I don't know that DVD.'

I consider explaining that no one uses DVDs anymore but decide to save that lesson for another day. I hold up a packet of fruit logs and a packet of Tim-tams.

'Do we need these?'

'Ah, you already know my weakness. Aki used to ration my biscuit intake. Only one with every cup of tea.'

'I think we can stretch the budget to two.'

In the cleaning aisle, Oji busies himself reading the labels on the back of the bottles to find which product is best for the new shower stall he had installed a few days ago.

Looking down the aisle, I notice a little girl staring. She is about the same age as Millie but may as well be from a different planet. Her clean blonde hair falls around her face in loose curls, her skin, pale and freckled. She wears a neatly pressed purple dress with a long sleeve white cotton shirt underneath. When I smile at her, she buries her face in her mother's pants leg.

'Mummy,' she tugs on her mother's arm.

The slender woman in designer blue jeans with a similar complexion, brushes the child off, reaching at the toilet rolls on the top shelf.

'Mummy!' the girl shouts again.

'What?' the mother snaps.

'Why do those people look funny?' the girl asks pointing at us.

The mother's face glows red in horror as she dropped the toilet rolls into the trolley.

'Christina!' she hisses. 'You don't say things like that!'

'Why not?' the girl whines. 'It's true. Their eyes go like this…' she goes to press her fingers to the corner of her eyes but her mother bats them down.

'Christina!' she shouts, and then turns to us. 'I'm so sorry… I don't know where she gets these things from…'

I don't know what to say. The girl's gesture brings back playground taunts, long buried. I am startled to find them still there; hidden like urchins in the shallows, dormant, but ready to inflict a sharp sting when stirred.

The girl's backpack is decorated with pictures from May Gibbs' *Snugglepot and Cuddlepie*. I remember the book from primary school – the fear struck in my classmates at the brown and hairy Banksia Men – the way I was never allowed to be Ragged Blossom in the playground. I never knew which character I was supposed to play, so I just sat in the sandpit ladling the grey silt into my bucket. When I tipped the bucket over, my creations slid formlessly back to their source, never retaining shape. When I told Jill about the sneers I received, she told me the old adage about sticks and stones – to ignore them – but she didn't understand. She didn't look like me. I wished for my father.

The mother grabs her daughter and drags her away by the hand. Down the aisle, a man in a high-vis shirt listens in. Tan skin, dark hair, dark eyes. He doesn't look like he is from here, either. He raises his eyebrows with a smirk in my direction and shakes his head. Oji looks up from the label he is reading and gives the man a wave; he waves back as he turns his trolley in the other direction.

'I think this one will do the trick,' Oji says placing a spray bottle in the trolley.

We continue on to the frozen goods section.

'Who was that man?'

'Diego. He did some levelling on the land for us when we first arrived. A very nice man.'

'And that woman with the little girl? Are people here always like that?'

'No,' Oji replies. 'Yes. Well, sometimes. It's not the most multicultural place, you've probably noticed. Diego is from somewhere in Latin America, and he's the only person I've met who isn't from here.'

He stops in front of the freezer and grabs four bags of stir-fry greens.

'Still…' I object, but I'm not sure what I expect him to do or say.

He holds up the packets of frozen vegetables.

'If you use the right sauces, you can't really tell the difference from the fresh ones.'

In the kitchen, Oji washes the dirt from under his fingernails while I gather the ingredients for Okonomiyaki: the savoury Japanese pancakes with salty, sweet sauce that I love.

'Your father always said I made this better than anyone.'

'Well, that was before you taught me.'

Oji laughs. 'We'll see if you're a good apprentice.'

I sift the flour into a large plastic bowl.

'Peter Kenney called yesterday,' Oji says as he cracks an egg. 'I had to tell him the news. Of course, he was very taken aback. I didn't organise a funeral because… well, I didn't have it in me, and most of Aki's colleagues and friends are still in Japan. So, I didn't think to call Peter. I suppose I should have…' He picks at his fingernails.

'Who's Peter Kenney?'

Oji explains that, when my father arrived at Russell Island, he was no longer working in any official capacity, but he connected with the local wader-bird monitoring group to offer his services.

He had used their data from time to time over the years. The president, Peter Kenney, was delighted to receive the call. Most members were retirees. It had been a long time since they had a real scientist in their midst. Scarcely resourced, their surveys extended along the southeast coast of Queensland, and Peter welcomed the addition of the island site to the pool of data which they collected and fed on to universities and interested research groups.

'He wanted to know if I would be continuing the surveys.'

Oji pours the eggs into the flour, and I start to beat, raising my voice over the clack of the whisk.

'What did you tell him?'

'I said I wasn't sure. I don't do very well walking long distances. I don't think I could commit, especially with all the work still to be done here... Unless you'd like to?'

That catches me off guard. I have never done any fieldwork. I don't like the dirt, or all the things that can bite, and potentially kill you. I think my mother was secretly disappointed when, as a child, I much preferred to flick through books by Alfred Russel Wallace, my namesake, than emulate his adventures.

Jill looks back fondly on her research days, and I am sure that her pristine appearance is just a way to distance herself from what she gave up. She probably would have loved it if I had followed in her footsteps.

I picture a beeline of explorers walking through dense undergrowth. Jill leads in khaki coveralls relaying the Latin names of the flowers she passes; my father meanders off to the left looking up through binoculars. I scurry at the back, trying to keep up, tripping on tree roots. Mud sprays up my legs and dries quickly in the heat. We walk deeper, and as we do, the trees slowly dissolve, dropping pixel by pixel like a distorting image on a computer screen, until my parents are engulfed and the ground transforms into a stark and windy bay.

In my daydream, I am left standing alone, looking down a long desolate shoreline. I walk towards a solitary shorebird, the water lapping at the soles of my leather boots. Drawing closer, the bird looks up at me but doesn't move away. I feel a deep sense of calm standing next to it. We both turn and watch the bay undulating from the horizon.

'Earth to Wallace,' Oji chuckles.

'Sorry,' I reply.

'So…?'

'So…' I stammer, scooping the shallots and cabbage into the mix.

'So, would you like to help?'

The image of the bird lingers in my mind. 'Sure. Why not?' Oji beams.

'Good, good. I'll give Peter a call tomorrow. I'm sure he will be very happy to hear it.'

I take out a small bowl to mix the sauce.

A large rhinoceros beetle slips in through the sliding door left slightly ajar. Its wings vibrate loudly as it flies into the walls and the ceiling. Oji tsk-tsks with sympathy. The insect drops to the ground. Oji bends down, groaning with the strain. The beetle retracts its limbs. Oji scoops the shiny black carapace into an upturned glass, cupping his hand over the top. Spurred to life, the beetle's pronged head butts into Oji's palm in a flurry. A trill escapes between his fingers like a muted choir of wind whistling through treetops.

Beyond the screen door, Oji removes his hand and the beetle's swift wings lift it up from the glass. It hovers for a moment, before gliding effortlessly away, becoming a smaller and smaller speck on the quiet canvas of new night.

3

The sign for Sandy Beach is weathered and chipped. The lettering is carved into a piece of driftwood nailed across two stabilising planks, dug deep down into the earth on a slant.

Over the flats, towards the mass of trees on the other side of the inlet, I can't quite reconcile the name with what I see. Sections of white sand teeter towards the definition of a beach but require lengthy stretches of the imagination to fit the title. Sandy Beach sits at the opposite end of the island to the jetty where the ferries dock and is as far as you can travel on the island without driving into the bay.

Oji told me this morning that the locals banded together a few years ago to bring sand from the mainland by the truckload. They spread it over the surface of the dark tidal mud to make the space more appealing. Now, on the weekends, families happily chatter on the banks while the children wade in the shallows.

'As happy as pigs in… mud!' he chuckles.

I am yet to hear Oji swear.

Sitting on a picnic table looking out to the opposite bank, I see the man in high-vis from the supermarket eating a sandwich. He sees me and waves. I am not used to this kind of small-town cordiality. I hesitate, not sure if I am supposed to wave back, or go over and say something to him. I look over my shoulder to see if he might be waving at someone else.

'Yes, you,' he shouts, and gestures me over.

Torn jeans, an old t-shirt, oily skin. I feel self-conscious and smooth down my hair as I make my way to the table.

'You're new here, aren't you?'

Up close it's hard to tell how old the man is, but I guess he is closer to Jill's age than mine. He has deep crow's feet, and a scruff of brown whiskers flecked with a few bristles of grey.

I nod.

He extends a hand. 'Diego.'

I shake. 'Wallace.'

'Your first name?'

'Yes, my parents were cruel like that.'

'No, it's a nice name,' he assures. 'Different, but better than those common names like Jessica, or Amy, or Sarah.'

I grimace at the sound of my friend's name, and he mistakes my look for disagreement, laughing.

'What are you doing here?' he gestures to my backpack.

'Oh, nothing. Just, some… just some bird surveys. My father was working here, but…'

I don't know how to begin explaining to a complete stranger that I don't know what happened to my father.

'Yeah,' Diego nods. 'I heard about that. So, you're Aki's girl. Sad, really sad. He was a good guy.'

I should have known that in a place like this everyone would know more about my father than me.

'Anyway,' Diego rises to his feet and we stand eye to eye. 'I have to get back to work.'

He points at the machinery down the beach on one of the vacant lots.

'Nice meeting you,' he shakes my hand again and encloses it with his other hand. 'I really am sorry about your father. Maybe I'll see you around.'

I nod, words caught in my throat.

He turns with a wave and strides away, whistling a tune I don't recognise.

'Wait,' I shout but it comes out hoarse.

Diego turns back.

'You know what happened to him?'

'Who?'

'My father.'

Diego looks sheepish, 'Look, I won't say anything to anyone.

I'm not part of the island gossip mill, I promise. I just happened to be nearby the day it happened. Oji needed my help…'

I search for the words to explain that I don't even know, but he takes my silence as a cue to keep moving.

'Sorry, I really do have to go.'

I nod and turn back towards the water to hide my embarrassment. 'Okay. See you around.'

The flats are empty aside from a few birds that stalk in slow circles in the distance. The wet ground sticks to my shiny new Doc Martens as I trudge on, and I try not to think about the dirt settling into the grains of leather, or how many Euros they cost me. I pull my feet up with loud sucking gurgles as I go. My fringe sticks to the sweat on my forehead. I wipe it away with my sleeve, but the salty itch remains. A mangrove tickles my ankle, and I jump.

I see the curlews in the distance scooping their heads down towards the mud, prying fat beads from the sand with their beaks. Approaching the tideline, there are hundreds of blue hermit crabs scurrying away. Shells and chitinous limbs clink like the wind chimes hanging on the verandahs of the nearby weatherboard houses. I stop for a moment and watch as the crabs move as one spreading mass, spilling over the mud like a bag of marbles. When I step too close, they sink down into their tunnels.

Forgotten vessels bob in the shallow water, crumbling roofs of tin and tarpaulin falling away. Reaching the curve where the curlews stand, I keep my distance, just like Peter told me to on the phone.

'As nervous as chooks at Christmas,' he said of the curlews. 'The biggest of the shorebirds, but nothing but a bunch of chickens.'

Peter really was excited that I would be continuing the surveys.

'A chip off the old block 'ey? Good to see, good to see!'

Placing my backpack down in the prickly spinifex, I take a seat on an abandoned upturned bucket with dark red-brown smears. The sickly odour of fish guts hangs in the air. The land snakes down around a thin bank dense with mangroves, before opening up to another clearing separated by an inlet. I take my father's binoculars from my bag and lift them to my eyes.

Across the adjacent mudflats there are six more curlews. Closely assembled shapes, their bodies are sloping and angular like the newly arrived cranes along the foreshore where the ferries moor. I hone in on one. It looks stringy and sickly. With feathers hatched in a saw-tooth pattern, from a distance the bird appears drab – two-toned – but on closer inspection there are multitudes of browns and greys. The lighter feathers on its breast are surprisingly varied, too, like the swatches for white house paint that Oji brought back from the hardware store.

I fill in one of the count tables from the pack that Peter sent to me by express post on Monday. It still took three days to arrive. Temperature, time, numbers, observations. The bird that I am watching is startled by the sound of machinery backfiring on the nearby block of land behind the mangroves. The churning engines and loud voices of the tradesmen cut across the stillness as lopped trees are loaded into the tray of a truck. The bird spins its head and opens its wings wide revealing bands of rufuous and mahogany – each feather with a milky tip.

I look at the page in the information booklet outlining the bird's flight anatomy. Each membranous wing conceals a harp of bones.

Supcracoracoideus.

The bird's muscles contract in an upstroke, suspended for a moment, before slowly pushing its wings down.

Pectoralis major.

Striated cambers of each wing narrow out to points. An exaggerated sternum puffs out in a large bow. The awkward shape makes flight appear nearly impossible, but I know, having recently been suspended in many cocoons of heavy metal, that appearances are nearly always deceptive when it comes to flight.

The noise subsides, and the bird lowers its wings.

I want to ask this curlew about my father. Could it have been a field accident? Did he slip and fall? Was his heart too weak? The bird turns towards me, and I see something like a hint of recognition in its eyes. I am not sure why, but my heart skips a beat.

Its slender neck slopes down again, like a branch batted by the wind, and I have a sudden desire to be on the adjacent beach, digging my own beak down into the mud in search of food; my legs curling at the knee with long angular steps; my head scooping and arching through the air in response to the rough whisper of engines.

Another loud crash from the building site, and this time the curlew sets off in leaping strides, bounding half a dozen steps before taking flight.

Layers of steel clouds obscure the sun.

From reading the pamphlet, I know now how much those wing beats cost. The birds are feeding for sixteen hours a day, buffering their bones with bags of fat for the 10,000 kilometre migration back to their breeding grounds. Every movement can mean the difference between landing safely or falling depleted into the ocean. Their feathers aren't waterproof. They can't swim. Without webbed feet, they only survive in the places between land and sea.

I watch the curlew fly and think how amazing it is that a creature can have the strength to travel the distance to the moon in its lifetime but still be so fragile. More follow, releasing guttural squawks as they go. They pass overhead, feet tucked neatly to the undersides of their bodies, as round and smooth as the hulls of boats. Dark silhouettes fall across the mud.

'Where is home?' I whisper.

There is no answer in the swooshing of wings, just a procession of shadows sailing on.

The newly constructed deck prickles as I pace. Not yet sanded, splinters of pine press into the soles of my feet. Sarah's name flashes on my phone screen, and I press the green button. Tonight is about the fifteenth time she's tried to call, and I finally answer. I want to hear her voice. Phone reception on the island is always poor but even more so when it's overcast. Just beyond the backdoor is the only place I can get a clear signal. The old plastic verandah roof has been pulled down to make way for a new metal one; I look up at the flat charcoal slab unmarked by stars. Our conversation is awkward at first – greetings, pleasantries. But we soon relax into our usual comfort.

'What does the sky look like at night?' Sarah sighs. 'I haven't been out of the city for so long.'

'It's cloudy tonight, but usually it's pretty spectacular.'

'If you don't come back soon, I might have to come visit.'

'I don't think you'd like it; it's pretty boring, really. There aren't even any restaurants. Unless you count the Chinese place near the IGA, but I haven't seen it open yet. It's like everything here is in between; even the people don't seem to be sure if they are coming or going.'

'You've been there almost a month. There must be something you like about it.'

'Yeah, it's peaceful, I guess. And I'm keeping busy.'

Sarah clears her throat, and I can picture her, head tilted to one side, phone propped between her ear and shoulder, rubbing the base of her neck mechanically until the skin flares red like she always does when she is anxious.

Sarah sighs into the phone, 'I miss you,'

'I know,' I mutter. 'I'm sorry.'

I remember being five years old when Sarah and her mum moved into the apartment next door to my grandmother's. In our primary school years, we would go to the park around the corner after school. The big jacaranda hung low. During Spring, we climbed across an enchanted kingdom, hovering above purple clouds. Sometimes, Sarah's long hair caught on the branches so that the hardest and softest shades of brown became one mound of tangles. I would patiently help her untwist the strands without pulling too hard.

'We are princesses in this purple world,' Sarah would whisper in delight.

I know the jacarandas are in season right now, which only makes me more nostalgic.

'How's work?' I ask.

'Oh, you know, the same as always. Fashion labels are still peddling androgynous, non-descript exoticism as the new black. You could be the poster girl for the brand I'm working with at the moment.'

I laugh. 'Thanks.'

Sometimes, I regret entering into a relationship with Sarah a year and a half ago. At the time, it seemed like what we both wanted – for me, Sarah was the most comfortable place in the world – but I eventually realised that I couldn't forge the kind of romantic love that she deserved, and I wanted more for her than I could give. Now, I wish we could go back to how it was before.

'You need a new job.'

'Not all of us can just drop everything whenever we want.'

The last month of our relationship felt like the last day of a long holiday where no matter what activities we did, everything was overshadowed with the sense of an ending. It was like carting suitcases down a busy main street, killing time in a café or cinema; it was like arriving at the airport before the check in desk has even opened in the hope that the whole process might be hurried along. It wasn't hurried along though. We drew it out. Tried to squeeze every ounce of joy from our time together, until all that was left was a pile of snapshots.

Eventually, I graduated, and desperate for an escape, broke things off and booked my trip to Europe alone, using some of my inheritance from Grandma Sue. Jill was certain that the whole relationship was just a phase and was happy to encourage me to go.

Sarah said she understood. She even went with me to the airport to wave me off at the gate, but I knew that as soon as I was gone, she would be holding back tears while eating an expensive chocolate brownie at one of the glossy chain cafes in the airport lounge, before going to the gym to work it off on the treadmill.

The downside to being in a relationship with a lifelong friend is that even when you're apart, you can predict their every movement. Sometimes, during my trip, I laid awake at night imagining Sarah sitting behind a keyboard at her advertising job, thinking about all the places she wasn't, biting her lip.

Sarah clears her throat.

'Can I get you to do me a favour?' I ask.

'Sure.'

'Do you think you can check my post office box and return my postal vote? I forgot that it's due this week.'

Earlier in the day, I was reminded of the marriage law postal survey by a radio interview with the leader of the opposition. I hammered louder to block out what he was saying but heard enough to know that I didn't want to miss my opportunity to contribute.

'Do you want me to mark yes or no?'

The tone of Sarah's voice hurts.

'Yes, of course. Why would you ask me that?'

'Well, after conversations we've had, I wasn't sure.'

'Just because I don't want the opportunity for me, doesn't mean that I don't want it for anyone.'

'I'm sorry. I know,' Sarah's voice softens. 'I just miss you. It's making me crazy.'

'Yeah, I miss you too. I just have a lot going on right now. And I've been meaning to talk to you. What happened before I came here...'

'I know, I know...' Sarah cuts me off, not wanting to hear what I have to say.

Suddenly, I regret answering my phone. It's not the first time I have tried to lean on Sarah when I know I shouldn't. I think about when I returned from my trip, and I felt lost. I was shaken by the news about my father, so I grasped for Sarah. In her bedroom, white sheets and white walls gave the appearance of convexity, a hollow orb containing us. There, my life felt contained and complete. We sat propped up in bed with fingers entwined.

'What's wrong?' Sarah asked.

I chewed my nails, even though I knew she hated it. 'Do you remember when you taught me the word Daddy?'

'No, I didn't know I had.'

I spat a chunk of fingernail into my spare open palm, and Sarah grabbed my other hand so I couldn't put my fingers back into my mouth. I rolled to face her.

'We were doing a jigsaw puzzle in your living room when you declared that your daddy was coming to take you camping for the weekend. I went home and asked Jill what it meant.'

Was it the name of the man who appeared every second Saturday in a blue ute and dropped Sarah home on Sunday evening with a head full of sugar, so that her stories of the weekend rolled off her lips so fast and excitedly that I could barely keep up?

Jill explained that everyone had a daddy, even if they didn't come to visit. She said that I was composed half from her, and half from a man who left when I was too small to remember.

'Sometimes I wonder what it would be like if I never heard you say that word. What if I didn't know he was in me?'

'What do you mean?'

'What if I'm like him?'

What if I will always run away and leave a wake of pain behind is what I really wanted to ask.

Sarah ran her hand through my hair, the feeling of her touch so familiar it could have been my own.

'Don't worry so much. You aren't anything like him.'

'How do you know?'

'I know you better than anyone.'

'But it's like I can feel it.'

She couldn't tell then that I was already gone. She held onto hope.

Sarah gripped my face and brought it directly in front of hers, staring into my eyes deeply. 'Nope, you're still just you.'

Her hands ran over my body squeezing, prodding, tickling. I squirmed, laughed.

'Stop it! I'm being serious!'

I wrestled free of Sarah's grip and climbed out of the bed. 'I guess I better go home. I have to pay my bill before they cut off my phone. And I have to decide if I am going to take Oji up on his offer.'

'Do you think you need to go to the island? You just got back.'

'Yeah, I want to.'

'Why can't you sort everything out from here?'

'There's still so much I don't understand.'

Sarah sat up in the bed, her slender breasts accented through her baggy white t-shirt, her brown hair that was wild and curly in childhood, cropped short around her face. She didn't say anything else, but, beyond the silence I could hear the distant hum of waiting, like an engine always in neutral. My chest tightened with guilt, but I pretended I didn't notice the change in her expression and bent down to kiss her cheek. She raised her chin upwards, lingering. I turned and walked through the doorway, leaving it ajar.

A month in, I still barely understand more than I did then. I haven't been able to broach the subject with Oji – the more time passes, the harder it seems. I know it is just one question, but the words always get caught. Maybe it is because I like Oji, and I don't want to upset him. Or maybe, I don't really want to know. Maybe knowing will cement the fact that my father is gone, and I don't feel ready to let go of what I never got to hold.

The phone line crackles with interference.

Sarah's broken voice cuts through. 'Sorry, I can't hear you properly, are you there?'

'Yes, I'm here. The line is really bad, though. It's about to start raining. I should probably go anyway. I don't really know what else to say.'

The trip to the island deferred any further discussion we might have had about our relationship, and I hoped a little extra space and time might resolve things.

'I know we're not getting back together,' Sarah mutters. 'I just wish there was something else.'

'There will be,' I assure, trying to convince myself, too.

There is a loud crash from the kitchen and through the glass door I see Oji standing over a dropped box of cutlery. Dozens of knives and forks spread across the floor projecting lasers of light. I am reminded of Mona Rey's terrible installations in my graduate exhibition. The curatorial majors were paired with an artist, and we had to create a one-night only showing. Mona constructed her metal objects in the courtyard at the centre of the university, while I projected floral paintings by Clara Peeters and Judith Leyster onto the buildings. We said that it was a comment on constructions of femininity across time, although we didn't really know what that meant; Oji's dropped forks probably have stronger convictions.

Oji looks out and laughs. 'The bottom of the box was damp. Lucky, the new cabinets arrive soon.'

I laugh back at the old man, impossible to rattle.

'What's so funny?' Sarah asks.

'Oh, nothing, I'm sorry. I have to go help Oji clean something up. But I'll talk to you soon, okay? I really will – I promise.'

I hang up the phone and go into the house where Oji is picking up the cutlery and putting it into a plastic container.

'Let me do that,' I say.

A battered Toyota Hilux clunks to a halt on the rocky embankment.

Peter Kenney clambers down from the step of his ute, grabbing at the doorframe for stability as his knee joints seize up. He swears, kicks at the red dust, and slams the door. Peter is small and wiry. His ripped jeans and flannelette shirt hang loose – his wide brimmed leather hat droops low over a face that is weathered like a garden gnome tucked behind a shrub and left to the elements for many years. Peter twists his neck awkwardly to deter a mosquito from landing on his face.

'Bastards,' he mutters.

He pulls some bamboo poles and a bag full of nets, tracking devices, and tools from the back of the ute, handing one pole to me, and carrying the rest himself.

'Can I help with more?' I ask, but he has already taken off at a brisk speed.

We make our way down from the car towards the Sandy Beach shoreline. The incoming tide covers most of the muddy banks so that only the light sand is exposed.

'It's a bit of a swamp this place, the mosquitoes are bloody shocking, but it's got something nice about it at this time of day.'

'Yeah.'

The boats that were beached now bob in the water. Faded colours and cracked hulls, the sun low in the sky.

I look over at the picnic table, but Diego is nowhere in sight.

Four upturned tinnies, recently painted white, are pulled up onto the dunes: the moored daydreams of some local entrepreneur. Everyone here has a plan in the making. Everywhere, the smell of drying paint.

'It's best to get the birds at their roosting site when the light is dim and the tide is high,' Peter says. 'Shorebirds have really good eyesight, so in full daylight they usually just avoid the nets.'

We trudge, boots and legs covered in the khaki waders that Peter brought with him. We continue around the bend from where I sat last time, through the knee-deep channel of water, and stop on the adjoining beach. A few birds are already gliding down to the banks, turning their heads to survey their strange visitors.

'Alright, we better get moving,' Peter barks. 'You take that pole twenty meters down that way and put it in the ground like I told you.'

I nod, trying to recall the lesson that Peter offered in the short drive from Oji's. At about the right distance, I angle my pole and look over to see Peter's already jutting up towards the sky, his sinewy body bending over the mound of netting. I burrow the pole into the sticky earth.

Peter walks towards me holding the edges of the net in each hand. He fastens it taut to the pole, creating an almost invisible sheet. The fine gauze shimmers.

'Now we just wait a bit,' he says. 'Easy 'ey?'

'Yeah, so far so good.'

Sitting on a nearby piece of driftwood, Peter pulls a thermos of coffee out of his backpack, fills two metal cups, and hands me one.

'Thanks.'

A chainsaw from Diego's job site lets out one final screech before powering down for the day. A lorikeet passes and a stream of droppings land next to Peter's foot. He scrubs the greenish liquid into the dirt with his boot.

'Close one,' he says, taking the last sip of his coffee. He lets out a loud sigh of satisfaction. 'Worst ways to spend an afternoon, if you ask me.'

'Yeah, thanks for bringing me.'

'Take after your old man, then?'

'Maybe,' I shrug. 'I didn't really know him.'

'He was a good bloke. Serious at first. A bit of a tough nut to crack. But a good sense of humour underneath that shell once you got through it.'

Good. That word again. I wonder what was so good about my father. It's not usually a word used to describe a man who abandons his infant child.

'Did you know him well?'

'We first met way back in 90... 90 something? He was here on a research fellowship at the uni. I was just a casual bird watcher then. After I retired, I started volunteering more of my time to the society. Then, when Mat moved back, we did a bit of monitoring together. He started pooling data over here on the island, and he was sending me some counts before he...'

Peter pauses and watches the whistling kites in the distance. I lean in eagerly, but he just fidgets.

'Well, you know. Anyway, we always chatted a bit here and there. He was very passionate, and a pro at what he did. Made more progress in understanding migrations than anyone else I can think of. If there was a quality paper written in the last thirty years, then his name was probably on it.'

'What do you mean?'

'His banding work, his tracking, his diet studies. He really shed a lot of light on where the birds are going. How long they are staying. Where they are stopping. I'm no expert myself, but from what others in the group tell me, he was one of the best.'

Looking at Peter, I think he must be nearing seventy. His body wears the marks of a life of sun and labour. I wonder why he isn't sitting at home with his feet up on the coffee table while reading the race form or setting sail on a cruise ship to an exotic but not so distant tropical island, like so many other retirees.

'And why do you do it? This work, I mean?'

Peter looks over as a few birds approach the beach. They glide wide of the net and land on the mud.

'I grew up in these parts. I remember when I was a kid, and every Spring the beach near my place on Moreton Island was full of birds. Now, there are a lot less of them, and the timing is all out of whack too… I dunno. I guess I might not be the sharpest tool in the shed, but I like to think that together we might be able to understand enough to fix some of what we are doing to them. I'm retired and my wife passed away a long time ago, so I've got enough time on my hands.'

Peter stands up to get a better look at the birds approaching, checking his watch.

'The wader group I work with is small, but we do what we can and feed all our data back to the university. Mostly I do it because I've got grandkids now. I want to be able to show them what I saw growing up. There's something magic about it, you know. Watching these birds arrive in massive flocks, feed, rest, and then disappear. Then the following year, the same ones are back, and their chicks. For me, it's a bit of a measure of time, and, as I get older, I guess time feels more and more important.'

I nod and wonder if my father felt the same way about time. Whether he gave any thought to how I perceived it. Why he never wanted to show me the magic that Peter so desperately wants to share with his grandchildren.

Peter puts the thermos in his bag as three curlews travelling closely together fly into the mist-net. Entangled, they emit short, sharp whines, twisting their wings against the snare.

'Bingo!'

Peter rises to his feet and rushes forward as another four birds fly directly into the net.

'We don't want to leave them there too long. They get a bit distressed, so we should get them down right away. They look good and healthy, mostly. Except that one,' he points at the skinniest of the flock. I recognise the bird I watched during my first count. 'We should be able to fit three devices on this bunch I reckon, and I'll fit the others back on the mainland.'

I stand, unsure of what I need to do. I follow Peter's lead, taking the net down from its fixings while keeping the birds contained beneath. All the time, I watch the gaunt bird; how it behaves differently to the others. It doesn't struggle, but seems to recline against the net, unphased.

'I'll talk you through the first one.'

Peter walks over and untangles one of the larger birds from the net holding the wings down firmly with his palms. The bird blinks its eyes; its chest puffs in and out rapidly; its long legs hang flaccid.

Peter gestures with his head. 'Grab one of the devices from the bag.'

I pick up one of the little black GPS trackers.

'Now,' Peter says, 'we want to loop the harness over the leg. Kind of like putting a pair of pants on a baby.'

I fumble to loosen the harness, dropping the tracker on the ground, before picking it up and fastening it with shaky hands.

'Sorry, I don't have much experience with babies.'

Peter grins. 'Good practice, then.'

The bird's feathers are wet, and there is an acrid smell.

'Now, tighten the straps around its thighs so the device sits flush on its back.'

I twist the harness around, so the square tracker is in the middle of the birds back between the wings, and pull the straps firm.

Peter places the bird onto a portable scale and scribbles some notes in a table in his field journal. The first column has the label AAA. He subtracts ten grams for the weight of the device and then jots the bird's weight in the second column. Its eyes are impassive black orbs. I try to determine what it might be thinking. I don't know what it must make of this strange inconvenience. The curlew walks a few steps away from its captors and, realising that it is free, scurries neck first into the scrub.

Peter inspects the remaining birds and selects the two largest, releasing the others. The skinny bird lingers behind.

'Is it okay?' I ask.

'Doesn't look it,' Peter says. 'Probably lucky to have made it at all. Predators'll probably take care of it over the next couple of days.'

I survey the bird sadly. The bones of its pelvis are protruding. It looks back at me, and I see that same familiarity in its eyes that I saw the last time. Then, I realise how I know that look. The image of my father sitting across from me at the Glebe café flashes in my mind. The curlew is staring at me with that exact same resigned gaze. My heart stops.

'Come on!' Peter yells.

I swing around and see that he is struggling to keep his grip on a wriggling bird. I hurry to help him fit the device, and, when I look back, the curlew with my father's eyes has gone.

'I know it isn't a huge number,' Peter says as we finish. 'But these things are bloody expensive. I am trying to get some more funding from the university, but we will see how we go.'

I am distracted, looking for the bird. 'Then what?'

'In the next few months, they will head off on their migration, and we will be able to see what happens on the way. Where they stop. If they make it. Maybe even eventually if they come back. I don't want to be pessimistic, but that might be unlikely. More and more are dying on their way because the places they are programmed to stop and feed at just aren't there anymore.'

'What do you mean?'

'Over developed. We're talking about places like China… Korea. The intertidal flats are being turned into all sorts of things. Progress doesn't slow down for a few birds. Not yet anyway.'

'That's so sad.'

'Yeah. I like to tell people to imagine it like this… Just say you're driving from Brissy to Alice Springs, and you've mapped out this perfect route where you can stop for petrol along the way, and then you're in the middle of the desert, and your red light is on, and the station that you pull up at has gone out of business. There isn't another one for miles. You'd be pretty buggered, wouldn't you?'

I nod.

'Well, it's a bit like that. Without fueling stops, the population has dropped by something like eighty percent in the last thirty years. A bloody tragedy, really.'

The sun is gone by the time we pack up the netting; there is only a thin sliver of crescent moon lighting the dusk. Peter fits a head torch and flicks it on. When he runs the light over the curlews, their silhouettes cast moon-shaped reflections across the sand.

The stars begin to emerge. If I join the dots just right, I can trace the outline of a long bird body, extending down from a lunar beak.

Peter scratches wildly at his neck.

'Let's get out of here before we're eaten alive.'

4

The sky is woollen with smoke and cloud.

It's a mixture of the lingering fire that has been burning over on Stradbroke for two days and the approaching storm that will extinguish the last flames. The smell has settled into the furniture, the sheets, our clothes.

Yesterday, Nev, at the service station, said, 'Pray that the rain'll hit tomorrow.'

But I'm not sure which God he wanted me to pray to. He doesn't seem like a holy man, but I suppose everyone becomes a little more pious in the face of nature.

Grandma Sue used to say that for her, God shimmered across the surface of the waves, and she never went to a church in her life. Maybe her God was the same as Nev's – synonymous with water. Whatever the case, it looks like Nev's prayers will be answered. A sheet of shadowy coolness has descended.

Oji is speaking on the telephone outside the back door. Last night, lying in bed awake, replaying the scene with the bird in my head, I decided that today I would ask him about what happened to my father. Perhaps, he knows something about that bird with my father's eyes and that's why he is being so vague. I wait for him to come back into the dining room.

It is the first time I have heard Oji speak Japanese. He speaks faster than when he is speaking English, not pausing to search for the right expressions. I listen in. I don't know what he is saying or to whom, but there is a soothing musicality to the sounds. If I shut my eyes, I could drift off to sleep.

I stop eating my cereal so the clinking of the spoon doesn't interrupt my eavesdropping. At first, the conversation is warm and bright, like two old friends catching up. Oji sounds happy.

Then after a few minutes, his tone changes. The sounds become short and staccato. There is a long silence, and for a moment I think the call has ended, but soon, the silence is broken – I can sense a goodbye coming.

For some reason, I imagine the person on the other end of the line is a woman. Perhaps it is in the way that Oji's voice is airy, radiating outwards, the same way that it does when he speaks with me. Maybe it's a sister, or a cousin. I try to picture what she might look like, but for some reason I can only conjure the woman who sat next to me on the plane ride from Sydney to Brisbane, her hair streaked with a patch of lightning grey, puffing up in a dome. I imagine that it's her absorbing Oji's words with care, and I realise how badly I want to know what they are saying to each other. I still know so little about Oji. I know what his favourite biscuits are, but I don't know where he grew up, whether his family gets along well, or who he talks to when he is sad.

Outside, Oji ends the phone call with a familiar melody of well wishes, perhaps accompanied by a promise to speak again soon. I hurry to continue eating my Weetbix before he comes inside, so he won't know that I have been listening.

'Everything okay?' I ask.

'Yes, yes,' he nods.

'Family? Back home?'

'Well,' he fidgets, slipping off his sandals, unaccustomed to a direct question from me; I am warming up for the questions I really want answered. 'It was my ex-wife, actually.'

I stop eating. 'Ex-wife! I mean... I'm sorry... I just didn't know.'

Oji shakes his head. 'Don't be sorry. We don't speak very often. She was just checking on how I am going here. She's a kind woman. Even after everything, she still cares very deeply about me.'

'That's good.'

Oji's shoulders slump and he sits in the chair opposite me, resting his chin on his hands.

'Right?'

'Sure, sure,' he agrees, but I can see that he is thousands of kilometres away. Seeing him like this, I am losing my nerve.

'Better than my parents. They never spoke after they separated.'

Oji nods. 'Yes, yes. Of course. You're right.'

I hurry to try to buoy his spirits. 'Tea?'

'Please,' he says, but still doesn't make eye contact.

He is staring off beyond the back garden, beyond the slender bars of melaleucas, light caught in the edges of the sloughing bark like old love letters held up to the sun.

I fill the kettle with water and the sound of the bubbles gyrating fills the silence.

'So, what did you tell her? Are you okay?'

I keep my back to Oji and try to push through the padded layers we've kept around our hearts until now. He doesn't say anything at first, but I can sense the words forming, so I wait.

'Yes, I told her that I'm okay. I told her that you're here. That it's nice to have the company.'

I stir the tea and open the biscuit jar.

'It's nice to be here.'

I place the cup and saucer down in front of Oji, four biscuits around the plate. Two chocolate, two fruit. He lets out a small laugh and picks one up, opening his eyes wide in delight.

'You know me too well already!'

I grin at the irony. He takes a bite and crumbs spill onto the plate.

'How long were you married for?'

'We were married for seventeen years, and I met your father towards the end of that time. After he returned to Japan. After you were born.'

The number catches me off guard. I wasn't expecting such a long time. I think of all the things that can fit into seventeen years. Primary and secondary school. Entire wars twice over. Britney Spears' whole career (pre- and post- the head shaving incident).

'What happened?'

'Well.'

He is gone again. His eyes drift to the piles of laminate flooring stacked in the living room.

'Perhaps, we can talk while we work. Those floors aren't going to lay themselves.'

I nod in agreement. I can sympathise with Oji. Perhaps, like me, he prefers to talk while he is doing something because the movement of his body helps to release the words, while at the same time relieving him from the penetrating eyes of the person he is talking to.

The storm moves closer.

It is so dark I could turn on a light, but I don't. We can talk more freely in the shadows. I push the stacks of flooring to one side while Oji sweeps the exposed concrete with a straw broom.

Hammer, handsaw, pencil, tape measure, safety goggles, gloves. The laminate floorboards connect with satisfying snaps. Tongue in groove, parallel to the incidence of light.

We follow the blotted and enigmatic instructions, occasionally improvising when we can't make sense of them. A slight tap with the hammer and clunk, click, clack, the slats slide in. Confronted with all this new information, I am more interested in my father's earlier life, than in what happened to him when he died. I know that I can't have both conversations, so I pursue this new thread for now.

'So, how did you meet my father?' I ask once we've gained some momentum.

Down on all fours, Oji grunts and jigsaws another piece into place. 'We were working at the same university. I wasn't an academic though. I was a translator in administration. I mostly translated different parts of the website into English.

Sometimes, someone would ask me to translate a letter to send to an American or British institution. I just did whatever was needed really. Some days there wasn't much work, and I dabbled in translating Romantic poems or portions of stories, but the English department had its own experts for that, so I just compared my translations with theirs once the course manuals came out. I always thought mine were better.'

A wry smile. Chisel, trimming knife, wrecking bar. The old skirting separates from the wall. Nails hammered flat. Debris flung into the rubbish heap off the back step.

'It wasn't a movie romance,' he fiddles in the toolbox. 'Things were different then. Every suggestion was loaded with fear. It was slow. We didn't even go for our first drink until we'd known each other for almost two years. And even then, it was a huge leap to move things beyond two colleagues sharing a few stories over hi-balls of whiskey. I was still married, but I suppose I had known all my life that I... well, that I like men. It just wasn't something that I could tell people then. Or there. And Aki had already lived here, had a relationship with your mother. You were already born. He didn't tell me about you until much later, but I could tell he had a complex history of his own. When his fingertips brushed over mine, everything in our past lives drifted away. It was... very special.'

I picture the dark space that Oji describes: an izakaya with only enough room for eight stools at the bar, the bartender bricked in by his bottles. My version of Oji's bar is only a pastiche; it is a King Street replica for Sydney hipsters. I have no real-life reference for it. Even though I have been tempted once or twice by the cheap flights, I have never been to Japan. Its neon lights and muted manners scare me. I have always been afraid of what I might find there, like in films when a character comes face to face with a doppelganger.

'Then, when he invited me to his apartment for a game of chess the following Sunday, I couldn't sleep all week,' Oji continues. 'We weren't children. We were men. We'd both lived lives. We both knew what we wanted.'

A large tear falls onto the freshly laid floor.

Ruler, pencil, a long grey line.

'I'm sorry,' Oji mutters and wipes his eyes.

The whir of the saw, the sweet smell of sawdust, and the short side fits perfectly into place. I don't want to upset Oji further, but I am still hungry for more information.

'And your wife. How did it end?'

Oji composes himself, clears his throat. 'I had to be honest with her. After all, she was the best friend I'd had in my whole life. She wasn't able to have children, so she blamed herself in a way. She thought that if we'd had a family, it would have been enough to keep me there. The norm then was that if a man were gay, he'd stay with his family and live a double life. It wasn't talked about, but it was a kind of unspoken rule. She gave me her permission, in a sense, but I did my best to explain how I didn't want that, for either of us. She couldn't really understand, but she let me go.'

'So, you started living with my father?'

Oji shakes his head and stops to finish his tea, the saucer resting precariously on a flimsy overturned box.

'Not until a while after that. I rented a flat at first. Aki and I kept working together for another year or so. We'd meet for lunch in the cafeteria. I didn't tell anyone else that I was getting a divorce. When work functions came around, I made up excuses about my wife being sick or visiting her parents. Meanwhile, Aki would send me documents to translate that weren't documents at all, but coded notes. On the weekends, we'd go on bird watching expeditions to the Kuina Forest or Yagaji Island, and he'd teach me about the different bird songs. What they meant. I loved seeing him in that environment. Away from the bureaucracy. Away from the lies we had to tell every day. He always seemed more at ease with birds than people.'

I sit crossed-legged on the floor, breathing in the smell of smoke still drifting in from outside. Is he at ease with the birds now? Before I can interrupt, Oji continues his story.

'Eventually, he secured a grant and moved to a different university. We moved in together after that. Both of our parents were already dead, and we didn't have any siblings, so there was no one we urgently had to come out to. We just lived a private life, and nobody bothered us. Not long after, I left the university too and took up work from home. I translated labels for companies. The instructions on shampoo bottles. The warnings on electrical items. It was dull, but I didn't have to lie anymore. I'd never been happier.'

'Did you have any friends?'

'Aki had contacts through his work, but they communicated mostly by email and phone. I had a few old colleagues. But not really. I had my words, and he had his birds.' Oji chuckles at the rhyme. 'Look, I'm a poet and I didn't even know it! Maybe those poems I translated rubbed some talent off on me.'

I shake my head. 'Has anyone ever explained the concept of a dad joke to you?'

The balmy shower starts to patter against the windowpanes.

'And then eventually you moved here?'

'Yes, but much later. Over a decade later. I think your father always missed this place. He was like the birds he studied – home spread across the globe – and a part of him always rested here.'

'What about you? Did you like it?'

'Yes, I still do. But especially when Aki was around. I liked it a lot. He made it possible to like just about any place. Looking through his eyes, I could see the layers of life. The complexity. Now, I worry that with time, the island will lose dimensions. Everything is starting to look a little flatter already.'

I am sad to hear Oji say that. For me, it is the opposite. Looking back at my life in Sydney, the city is a lithograph of grey buildings pasted onto a flat sky; the harbour, just another paper layer ripped carelessly and fixed to the foreground. The island has so many dimensions. Its rocky edges give the appearance of containment, but it extends in all directions: down into the brown silty soil, and the loamy red dirt – out into the fomenting sky with its stony clouds cracked open by bolts of brilliant silver – across the windcut bay, the glassy bay, the ever-changing bay. I can't imagine it in only two dimensions. Learning about my father from Oji, I can sense him in the air here, spilled like water colour over every part of the scenery.

The rain falls harder.

'We better close everything up so the floor doesn't get damp before we seal it off,' Oji says. 'That's enough for today.'

I know that he is talking about the work and the conversation. I am disappointed, but also grateful. When we stand up, I give Oji a hug.

'Oh,' he chuckles again, caught off guard.

He hugs me back. His skin is thin and soft, the weight of his body welcome.

'Thank you,' I say.

He holds me tighter. 'No, thank you.'

Our voices are just audible over the drumbeat of heavy drops on the roof. I can feel him trembling lightly, like a leaf suspended, but not yet falling.

> O, Curlew, cry no more in the air,
> Or only to the water in the West.

Sitting at the café by the jetty, I inhale the earthy scent that comes after rain. Crystals of water still cling to the low hanging leaves. The smoke in the air has cleared but the clouds persist. There's a name for the smell that is released by the dry soil when it gets wet, but I can't remember it. I'm sure my father would have known.

Yesterday, I found myself in his office, breathing in the smell of his books. I read over the lines of poetry that I copied from his collection into my notebook. Amongst the science books and natural history compendiums on his shelves I was surprised to find certain volumes of poetry: William Butler Yeats, Dylan Thomas, Henry Wadsworth Longfellow. As I flicked through, I discovered highlighted passages, always relating back to the curlew. A strong gust blows the trees, shaking droplets onto the pavement.

There is enough evil in the crying of wind.

I look down at my phone, trying to find out what the curlew meant to Yeats, but there is no signal. The wheel in the corner spins and spins. I stand up and hold the phone towards the sunless sky, hoping that some waves might be trapped under the cloud cover, or that the clouds will part and let a signal through. Arm outstretched, the page slowly loads, and I read that for him, the haunting cry of the curlew was about lost love. Maybe the poem was his attempt at turning the cry into a language he could understand. I think about the gaunt bird that I saw and wonder if I am like Yeats. Trying to relate something in nature to something human.

I so desperately want to see the bird again.

'You right?' Kate, the owner asks, as she collects the plates on a nearby table.

'Yeah,' I sigh, sitting down again, taking the last sip of my double strength latte. 'Just trying to get a signal.'

Kate's coffee really is the best on the island. A big step up from the two-kilogram tin of Nescafe at Oji's place.

'Ah yes, desperate for contact with the outside world! I think you've contracted island fever,' she says.

I laugh.

'Seriously!' she exclaims.

'I'm just tired.'

I like Kate. She is what Jill would call a free spirit. She pushes a frizz of dyed lilac hair back behind her hemp headband, wide hips swinging under her full-length tie-dye skirt. She wears an anklet with bells on it, so a faint tinkering scores her every movement.

She shakes her head. 'Don't be so sure.'

She tells me that last May she was going batty and hired a replacement for a month so she could visit her parents on the Gold Coast.

I've heard people talk about island fever – in the supermarket, at the post office – but I thought it was a joke. A symptom of living in close confines. Neighbours sticking their noses into each other's business. Not being able to leave the house without running into an ex. But I wonder if Kate is right. More than just thinking about the bird all the time, there are physical symptoms too. My whole body feels heavy, as though I am putting down roots, and every day that I spend here, they get a little bit deeper and harder to pull up. I think of the distance from the mainland again and can't shake the feeling that it's increasing. It's like the island is drifting further away from my home, my mother, my friends, and me with it.

Oji's Honda Civic idles into the car park and comes to a stop in the space just in front of the café. He hoists himself from the driver's seat and closes the door.

'Mind if I join you?' he asks.

'Of course not,' I smile.

He looks fresh in brown trousers and a cream button up shirt.

'Needed to get out of the house for a bit. The smell of paint is making me woozy.'

He faux wobbles on his feet, grabbing the edge of the table.

'Take it easy,' Kate laughs. 'I don't want you breaking a hip on my watch! The usual?'

'Yes, please.'

Oji sits down across from me and takes a newspaper from the satchel slung over his shoulder. He opens it to a half-finished crossword puzzle.

'A drop mixed before a dispersion,' he looks up, scrolling through an invisible catalogue of words. 'Eight letters.'

'I have never liked cryptic puzzles,' I reply.

Oji drums his pencil against his temple. 'They're good for the mind, and good for keeping my English sharp, even after all these years.'

I try to picture my father in this scene. Did he sit in this chair across from Oji? Was he any good at helping with the crossword? How did he take his coffee? Or did he prefer tea like Oji?

I tap my fingers anxiously on the table.

'Something wrong?' Oji asks.

'Hmm?'

I try to shake the poem from my head.

'I feel... I don't know, restless.'

Kate places a pot of tea down on the table.

'Oh, that,' Oji nods. 'Yes, that's normal. Island fever.'

'I told you!' Kate says gleefully.

Oji gives her a nod and goes back to his crossword.

'Because your crying brings to my mind, passion-dimmed eyes and long heavy hair.' I read a line under my breath.

'What was that?'

'Oh nothing, just reading out loud.'

Oji raises his eyebrows but keeps scribbling in the white boxes. When I keep tapping, he looks up again.

'Have you considered taking up exercise? Swimming. That's what I do when I start feeling the itch.'

'I don't know if you've noticed, but this isn't exactly Vanuatu. I'm not swimming in that sludge.'

Sometimes, I would swim in the Harbour beaches around Sydney, floating on my back watching the boats in the distance, the tanned and oiled chests of the rich skippers with unbuttoned white shirts glistening in the sun. I can't imagine doing that here though. I'd probably be taken by a bull shark, and the smell of the water would linger on my hair for a week.

Oji smiles. 'I meant at the pool.'

I shake my head. 'I don't know.'

I've never really liked exercise. Sarah used to make me go to the gym in the city with her sometimes, but I never knew what I was supposed to do with all the equipment. There were too many buttons to press. I felt like everyone was watching me as I beeped through the hundreds of settings.

I keep reading my phone while Oji works on his crosswords. Ferries come and go.

'I have one for you,' I say to Oji as he turns from the crosswords to the page filled with Sudoku puzzles.

'Mmm?'

'A clue. Or more a question. Because I don't know the answer.'

He looks up. 'Goodie. What is it?'

'What do you call that smell after rain?'

Oji inhales deeply.

'Pe-tri-chor,' he sounds out every syllable. 'A beautiful word, isn't it?'

I breathe in too, and the smell intensifies now that I can name it. 'Yeah, it is.'

'I like that,' Kate pipes up from two tables over where she is collecting the salt and pepper shakers. 'Give me a tic. Let me show you something.'

She goes inside and I can see her silhouette pass behind the counter, into the room beyond. She comes back holding a large rectangle. When she steps outside again, I can see that it's a canvas.

'Petrichor,' she repeats. 'Would be a good name for this one, don't you think?'

She holds up a mandala painted in the shape of a lotus flower. The segments between the intricate lines are shaded with subdued blues and greens. While the image is complex, it doesn't move me.

'Oh, yes,' Oji nods. 'Yes, yes. Beautiful.'

'Laura's latest.'

'Wallace is an artist, too,' Oji chimes.

'Not really,' I say.

Kate starts talking excitedly as if she hasn't heard me. 'That's fabulous. Laura and I have been talking about putting on a show. She paints here in the afternoon sometimes. Well, in the courtyard out the back. She's very talented. We were thinking an evening exhibition. Something small and intimate. Some music, maybe. Wine. Cheese. Something classy, you know? If you have any work to include that would be great. Maybe you can even sell…'

'I don't paint.'

Oji interrupts. 'But you did put on that show at university.'

'Really? We would love help organising!' Kate is leaning in now and I can smell her lavender perfume. 'I'm not as hip as I once was. You wouldn't need to paint anything. Maybe you could just give us a hand with the theming, the invitations, that sort of thing?'

I wonder if this would count as a job that I could report back to my mother. I am sure it's not what she had in mind when I graduated, but I don't know how I can say no. I don't exactly have a full schedule.

'If I'm still around, sure.'

Kate gives a little squeal. 'I can't wait to tell Laura! She'll be over the moon.'

The doorbell chimes and Kate rushes inside to take an order with extra spring in her step. I give Oji a stern look.

'What?'

'You know what.'

'I don't know a thing. Well, nothing more than what the crosswords ask me.' He gives me a smug smile. 'It will do you good. You might make some friends.'

'Why do I need to make friends? You don't have any friends.'

'But I'm an old man, and you're a budding young woman.'

'I'm not a flower.'

Oji bears his teeth in a cheesy smile. 'Perhaps not, but still as lovely as a rose.'

'Flattery won't get you anywhere.'

'Thorns, too,' he quips.

I laugh.

When the school bell rings, and Kate starts to stack the chairs, we take it as our signal to get back to work.

'I'll call you, Wallace.'

I give Kate a thumbs up out the car window.

'Look, you're friendlier already,' Oji grins.

At the house, the floor is nearly finished with just a few more slats to cut and insert at the edges before applying the seal. The space is open and airy; the new orange feature wall in the living room seems to suck the light in.

Oji goes straight into his bedroom and appears with a pair of blue swimming goggles.

'Swimming,' he reminds me. 'You can even borrow these.'

'You're full of ideas today.'

I take hold of the eyecups, pull the rubber strap over my head and adjust them on my face.

'Like a finely groomed fish!'

Puckering my lips, I suck my cheeks in and out. Oji laughs and leans against the wall.

'It's looking good,' I say.

'It is, isn't it?' he sighs. 'Like new.'

There is a sense of relief in his voice – of something shifting and falling into place.

The local swimming pool is open on Monday, Wednesday and Friday after school, and all day on Saturday and Sunday. Oji drops me at the front gate on his way to the nursery to buy a few more plants for the front yard.

'Do you want me to pick you up in an hour?' he asks.

'That's okay, I'll walk.'

The car rasps and sputters away. I enter through the open gate leading to the twenty-five metre lap pool. The squat oblong looks miniature compared to the Olympic size pool at my university swimming centre. I never swam there, but, when I walked past, I admired the way that the athletes glided through the water. I wondered how they got their hair dry before the next class. It all seemed like such an effort.

Digging in my pocket for coins, I pay $3.50 to the sullen teenager with dyed black hair and acne scars manning the turnstile. I can't imagine him wet. He looks as though he might dissolve in water. I bet he was put up to the job by a stern parent who cut off his pocket money when they found his secret stash of cigarettes or marijuana. He eyes me suspiciously.

'You new here?'

'Yeah, kind of,' I reply.

'Alright,' he says, shrugging his shoulders. 'It's cheaper if you become a member, but the president needs to be here for that, so you'll just have to pay full fee today.'

'No problem.'

He points past the closed canteen. 'The change rooms are back there.'

I am struck by the smell of chlorine. Inside the change rooms, the wooden benches are sticky with moisture; the pranged locker doors hang open. The scene reminds me of my high school locker rooms. Shy, I used to put my swimsuit on over the top of my underwear and, like a contortionist, wriggle my bra and underpants out from underneath. I repeat this trick now in case someone walks in. I am still self-conscious of my body. I pull on my black one-piece over my bra and underpants then stretch the elastic of my boy-leg briefs to their limits as I pull them down over my leg and slip the right foot through the leg hole. Then, I thread the fabric out the other side and down over my left foot. Next, I dig my hands inside the lycra around my back and unclasp my wireless crop top.

At school, Tina Vella used to mock me in her singsong voice when I did this same undressing dance before swimming class. 'Don't they get their gear off where you come from McKenzie?'

I never bothered to correct her. I could have told Tina that I was from the same place as her, but, instead, I let the other girls snicker and watched silently as Tina's full breasts lolled. Every swimming class and carnival after, I arrived early and changed in the toilet stalls. Now, looking at the contours of my shimmering black swimsuit, I feel as lean as an otter. I press my palms to either side of my waist and push until my fingers almost touch.

Stretching by the edge of the pool, I spot Diego, but this time he isn't wearing his high-vis. He is standing on the edge of the second lane from the end in swimming trunks. He reaches his arms high above his head, every muscle in his body tensing. He doesn't see me. Poised before the dive, he bends his knees slightly and propels into the air. The pool is so small that, once he pumps his body, he has almost reached the other end. He ducks under in a perfect somersault but doesn't push off the wall. Instead, he uses his arms to start moving himself forward right away.

Standing on the edge, I adjust Oji's goggles and pull them over my eyes. The pool glows pastel blue from the painted concrete hull. There is a cool rush into my ears as I dive. Arm over arm, I cut down the end lane. I find comfort in the shapes of the water and the way they twist around me as I swim. Beneath the surface, sounds become replicas of themselves, like bells struck far away. I connect to the count; the one, two, three, four; the patience for breath; the trust in my blood. Then, the heady rush before the gasp. The devouring of fresh oxygen.

Every now and again, when I turn my head to the left, I see Diego passing by – the only other inhabitant in my aquatic world. His motion generates sparkling wheels that spin through the water.

After thirty minutes, my muscles feel tired, but different to how they felt after a session at the gym with Sarah. Full like sponges; it becomes more difficult to stay afloat. I pull myself from the pool as Diego passes by. When he lifts his head for a breath, he gives me a wink.

As I'm walking towards Oji's place, a burnt orange Holden Commodore slows beside me, just like the 'Bogan Ferraris' Sarah and I used to joke about when the boys in our grade raced their cars up and down the foreshore in front of Maroubra beach. Jacob Mitchell always won. He had the same model and colour as the car idling next to me.

Diego leans across and shouts out the passenger window. 'Want a lift?'

He is nothing like Jacob Mitchell. No boyish spots. No bleached blonde tips. His hair is dark and curled, still wet.

'It's not that far,' I reply.

'Didn't really answer my question, so I'll take that as a yes.'

He flings the door open. My heart beats faster.

I lower myself into the passenger seat.

'Yeah, okay. It looks like it's going to rain again.'

Opaque clouds move quickly over the small patches of blue.

'Sure, that's why you got in.'

I blush and wind down the window.

'Stalking me, are you?' Diego asks with a smirk. 'First the grocery store, then by the beach, now the pool.'

'No,' I laugh nervously.

'Relax. It's a small island. If you say so, I'll accept that it's just a series of coincidences.'

I don't say anything. I look out the window as we pass by houses spaced at irregular intervals, mostly adjoined by vacant blocks. Many display For Sale signs with the smiles of real estate agents staring out. The radio starts to lose reception. I realise that I still haven't given him the address.

'I'm on Castle Drive.'

'I know, small island. I helped your dad and Oji with some work when they moved.'

'About the other day...'

'Look,' Diego says, cutting me off, 'I don't make a point of getting involved in other people's business. Forget I said anything.'

I don't want to forget, but he turns up the radio.

'Banger.' He nods his head in time to the Meat Loaf track and I roll my eyes.

'Seriously?'

Diego smirks as he thrashes his head.

We pick up speed and the warm air makes the chlorine on my skin tingle.

Diego turns the car off the bitumen, onto the rocky side road.

'Haven't you got a car here?'

'I don't know how to drive,' I confess.

I never really needed a car in the city. Jill did pay for a driving lesson when I was sixteen, but the instructor was a gruff old man who snapped whenever I asked a question. When I failed to brake in time for an orange light, he jammed his foot down on the passenger controls so hard that the brake pedal on my side pressed into the top of my foot. When I started crying, he instructed me to pull over. Sarah told me that her dad could teach me but I just said that I didn't want my license anyway; that driving was the largest contributor to CO_2 emissions. I took trains and buses instead. They ran on time often enough and went almost everywhere I needed to go.

'What!' Diego shouts in disbelief. 'How old are you?'

'Twenty-two.'

'That's outrageous.'

'Not really.'

'Yes, really!'

We approach the Queenslander propped up on stilts and bump to a stop at the bottom of the hill. The old stove is out next to the bins; the new white and purple petunias are already fringing the concrete driveway. It doesn't look so much like a construction site anymore.

Oji is on the deck, hammering a hat rack next to the front door. I suppose that it must be for Peter because no one else who visits wears a hat. Not that anyone else visits – unless you count the mailman. The last time Peter came, Oji grimaced when he laid his akubra on top of his boots.

Oji turns and waves. Diego waves back.

'So, I'll see you on Saturday morning for a driving lesson then.'

I open my mouth to reply, but he cuts me off. 'No ifs or buts: 9am.'

He honks his horn as the tyres spin in the orange dirt. I can see Jacob Mitchell in my mind, whooping and pumping his fist under streetlights haloed with salt.

I wipe my sweaty palms on my shorts and go inside, not looking back, just in case Diego catches sight of me in the rearview mirror.

5

The local RSL is filled with raucous chatter.

It's a squat brick building tucked off one of the paved roads and surrounded by bushland. Most of the buildings here look like they've sprouted up with the trees.

Oji and I sit across from each other at a cheap pine table eating grilled fish and salad. On the television mounted behind the bar, the man from the Bureau of Statistics stands in front of the camera ready to share the count.

I lean back in my chair.

'Not bad,' I say to Oji.

The food is better than I expected – flaky white fish crumbling under my fork – mustard dressing on the salad with just the right amount of vinegar. Today, the nation will hear the results of the marriage plebiscite, so Oji decided we should go out for a pre-emptive celebratory lunch. If he couldn't participate in the vote, he at least wanted to do his part with some positive thinking.

Nev Smith slams his empty beer glass down on the bar. 'I just wish he would bloody hurry up.'

From behind the stacks of dirty glasses, Barry McInnes turns up the volume. 'If there's any ruckus, I'll kick you out, the lot of you.'

Ben Wright stands up and taps his fork on his schooner. 'I'd like to make an announcement.'

The six men propped on stools fall silent.

Ben clears his throat. 'I'd just like to say that I'll buy a beer for the first bloke who proposes to Barry.'

An eruption of guffaws.

Behind us, Megan Riley and Lisa Johnson sip white wine. Megan works at the post office but must be on her day off.

Lisa rubs some lipstick off the rim of her glass. 'They say vote tampering was rife. You wouldn't know anything about that would you?'

'I don't know how anyone'd know anything about that. There were no identifying marks on the ballots or the envelopes.'

'And I suppose you checked first!'

'Shhhh,' Megan scolds.

Lisa lowers her voice. 'Just good on you, is all that I'm saying. Someone has to stand up for our family values.'

They clink their wine glasses.

I think about all the opened envelopes that Megan probably shoved at the bottom of the recycling skip.

Oji clenches his hands in his lap and turns his chair to face the television.

'What a farce,' Terry Bennett says to no one in particular as the men around him continue to joke and jostle. 'Why do they need to get married for anyway? Now they're on at the cake makers, and the celebrants and everyone else, too. Next, they'll be telling you it's discrimination not to pump the petrol for them, Nev.'

'Too right,' Nev raises his glass.

'I think Pauline's got the right idea,' Lisa adds.

I want to scream or at least stand and tell them all to shut up, but I just look straight ahead and sit perfectly still, as though someone is painting my portrait.

'And now the official results…'

Oji looks at me nervously.

'This is it,' I hold my breath.

The chief statistician's expression divulges nothing in the moment of silence that seems to stretch on and on.

'Yes responses 7,817, 247, representing 61.6% of responses.'

The woman translates in sign language behind him, her hands unfolding in a beautiful dance. Across the room, there is a mixture of groans and hoots. I know that we are predominately among the other 39.4%.

'What do you lot care for, anyway?' Barry shouts.

'Doesn't bother me,' Ben Wright says. 'People should be able to do whatever they want. It's a free country.'

Terry Bennett drops down on his knee in the middle of the floor. 'Hey, Baz, will you marry me?'

Barry rolls his eyes. 'Yeah, mate. My wife won't mind at all.' He takes a glass from the rack and nods at Ben. 'This one's on you, smart ass.'

The full glass plops down, foam spilling onto the counter. Terry gets back to his feet and flicks his tongue at Ben.

Oji leans across the table and gives my hand a tight squeeze. I squeeze it back. We smile, but keep our excitement concealed.

'The world is changing,' Oji says wistfully.

'Thank God,' I sigh.

My shoulders relax, and I sink into my chair.

I should call Sarah. I wonder where she is right now and whether she has someone to celebrate with. I think about her wrapped in the arms of another woman in the pub we like on Erskineville Road, and I don't feel sad or angry. I try to feel happy, but I don't feel that either.

'I wish your father was here to see this,' Oji says into his glass.

'Me, too.'

He shifts his weight and takes the last sip of his beer.

'You really loved him, didn't you?'

'Very much. Very, very much.'

Oji turns his attention to his hands, picking paint from the cracks of his palms.

The noise around us increases. Barry mutes the TV as it cuts to celebrations on Oxford Street then turns up the Nickelback track thrumming through the mounted speakers.

The white flecks of paint from Oji's hands fall like confetti onto the tarnished wood.

My phone vibrates in the centre console, and I look over at all the ignored notifications on the screen. My hands follow my eyes, and the car starts to veer to the left.

Missed call Jill

Missed call Sarah

Missed call Unknown

'Eyes on the road!' Diego scolds. 'My God, Wally, no wonder you haven't got a license. Lucky, we're only going about ten k's an hour.'

No one has ever given me a nickname before; the unexpected intimacy catches me off guard, but I quite like it. I redirect my wrists and screw my face up in embarrassment.

I groan and slow the car even more. 'I'm sorry!'

We bump along the rocky unpaved street, almost to a stop.

'Don't slow down!'

'Couldn't we do this in a parking lot or something? I feel like it might be easier on smooth ground?'

'No way; you aren't ready for other cars yet. Or they're not ready for you.'

I laugh.

'Now accelerate. Slowly. That's it. Foot on the clutch. Release. Slowly. And into second.'

I lift my foot off the clutch too rapidly and the car stalls.

Resting my head on the steering wheel, I sigh. 'I don't even want my license. Did you know that cars are the biggest contributor to CO_2 emissions?' I start to take off my seatbelt, ready to give up.

'I don't want your excuses!' Diego scoffs. 'And I think it's actually cows that are the biggest contributors to CO_2.'

'Well, I don't eat red meat, either.'

71

'Congratulations, Mother Theresa, but I'm not buying it. Let's start the car again.'

I groan and turn the key in the ignition. I rev the accelerator a little too hard as the engine stutters into first, but we start to move. This time, I feel the revs increasing, and carefully, slide into second gear.

'That's it!' Diego applauds.

He turns up the radio. Talking Heads rock anthem "Road to Nowhere" blares out, and Diego croons along loudly with his best David Byrne impression. Even at thirty kilometres per hour, I feel like we're flying.

'We know where we're we going, but don't know where we've been… Now third!'

I press my foot on the accelerator a little harder and edge up into third gear. When I coordinate my feet in time and hear the revs drop back obediently, I give a small shriek.

'I did it!'

'Yeah, you did!'

We're on a ride to nowhere…

We cross onto the bitumen road and turn right towards Sandy Beach. Heat steams up off the road, warping the air. The glare is so concentrated that it makes it hard to see too far ahead. I pull the sun visor down and confidently steer with one hand. I steal a glance at Diego looking out at the passing bush, elbow propped on the window frame, tapping his fingers on the roof. In the hard light, he is ruggedly handsome.

He catches me. 'What are you looking at? Eyes on the road.'

My face goes hot, and I look ahead.

'I bought some sandwiches and a couple of beers for lunch. Why don't you pull in up there?'

He signals to the patch of dirt by the picnic table and playground at Sandy Beach. The swings are wound around their A-frame so that they only hang a foot from the upper beam –

the red plastic slide is sun-worn and cracked.

'Drinking and driving. Wow. Good teacher.'

'The beers are for me. You're my designated driver, thank you very much.'

I roll my eyes. 'Right.'

I park the car without trouble, and excitedly lift my feet off the pedals, forgetting to shift into neutral. The engine clunks.

Diego says nothing, just shakes his head.

As I climb out of the car, sweat drips down the back of my knees. We sit at the picnic table under the shade of a scribbly-gum. I feel like I can almost read the messages encrypted in its bark. Diego cracks a beer can open, and it gives a satisfying hiss. He hands it to me.

'Here. You did good today. I'll drive from here.'

'Thanks,' I grin.

I don't usually drink beer, but I take a swig and the bitter liquid cools me at my core.

'Easy, tiger.'

I give a slight hiccup. Diego laughs, shakes his head again, and takes a sip from his own can.

For a while, the bush does the talking. Crickets rattle like slowly shaken maracas, while magpies warble a weary refrain

'Why did you move here?' I ask after a while.

'For this,' he says. 'There's nothing like this where I'm from.'

'What was it like there, in Colombia?' I ask.

'When I was growing up in Bogota,' he says, 'I made up for the absence of windows in my room with posters from *National Geographic* magazines. My favourite was of the Sydney Harbour Bridge.'

'Really?' I smile, thinking of the construction that I've seen so many times in my home city. Driving across the bridge every week made it a thing of utility. 'What did you like about it?'

'In that poster, I lost all my Catholic faith because the bridge was lit up against a dusk sky that was so clear it denied heaven.

I was sure I could see all the way to the edge of the universe in that sky, and there was not a single blemish on the nautical blue. The gloss on the print shone, and every time I looked at it, I was reminded of a world beyond the limits of my room – my city – a whole world beyond broken bricks and constantly checking over one shoulder.'

I've never heard Diego speak so poetically. His words make me rethink how I see the bridge – that colourless rainbow of metal arching over the harbour, its intricate frame holding the city together. 'That's a really beautiful way to describe it,' I say. 'Is that why you came to Sydney?'

'It is, but I couldn't make it there. It was too expensive, and I wanted something quieter. And there was a woman. But isn't there always?'

I nod. 'Yeah, right.'

I try to hide my inexperience with a casual remark and look over at Diego to see if it has worked, but he doesn't acknowledge me.

'How old are you now?' I ask.

'Jeez, Wally, don't you know you should never ask a man his age?'

I laugh.

'I'm thirty-eight,' he says, taking a gulp of his beer. 'Leaves a bad taste in the mouth, though.'

Static electricity from Diego's denim jeans makes the stray hairs on my thighs stand up. I can feel the space between us. I look away, towards the scrub. Mangrove fern, grey mangrove, river mangrove, orange mangrove, yellow mangrove, blind-your-eye mangrove, black mangrove, red mangrove. I try to match the names of the plants on the foreshore to the names in the book that Peter loaned me, but they all look too similar to tell apart.

Eventually, Diego's gaze is stronger and draws mine up. I lean in expectantly, but, all of a sudden, he pulls back.

'We should get back.'

Turning his face away from mine, Diego takes the last swig of his beer. He is close enough that I can smell it on his breath. He scrunches the can flat and without another word, stands up and heads back towards the car, tossing the aluminum disc into the bin as he passes. The clang of metal rings out, and the insects and birds seem to hold their breath. A thin veil of silence shrouds the beach.

Following behind, I close the car door quietly.

Diego's face is stiff and cold as we drive towards Oji's in silence.

A flying fox passes overhead dragging its heavy smell.

Walking from the pool back to Oji's, I slow down as I reach the memorial park. I think I might see Diego swimming, but it is just me and an old woman using a kickboard to stay afloat. She pushes the foam arrowhead out in front of her, the loose skin on her upper arms billowing.

I stop walking when I see someone moving next to the central garden bed. It is almost dark, but her carroty hair stands out against the shrubs. I cross the dried lawn. There are no gravestones to step around – just a few benches designated as sites for remembrance, and a ring of plaques along a low wall where ashes are kept.

As I get closer, I see that Milly is playing with a tatty Barbie doll. There are large chunks cut out of its matted blonde hair, and it doesn't have any clothes on. She whispers something to the doll that I can't quite make out, then laughs her piercing trill. I look around for Max, or a parent, but she is alone.

'Hi,' I say softly, careful not to startle her.

Milly turns her head and jumps to her feet. 'Wallace!'

Launching forward, she wraps herself around my leg.

Today, she is wearing a singlet that was white once, and a pair of boy shorts that hang too low in the crotch.

'Hi,' I pat her head. 'How are you?'

'I missed you!' she shouts not letting go.

I laugh and pry her arms off me. 'I missed you, too.'

She sits on the ground again, and I sit down beside her. 'What are you doing here?'

She points at the nearest plaque. 'Talking to my mum.'

Alison Hall. 1st of June 1985 – 24th April 2015.

I don't know what to say, but Milly isn't deterred by my silence. She talks almost breathlessly, like she isn't used to anybody listening.

'Mum says that she is glad that I have you for a best friend. She says that maybe you can show me how to do my hair in a braid like the one you had last time I saw you over there,' she points off towards the jetty. 'I told her how pretty you are.'

'Did you? That's very nice of you.'

I shuffle behind Milly and start to run my fingers through her knotted hair. 'So, you want a braid, huh?'

She nods.

I part her hair with my nail but pull my hand back in fright when I see small creatures darting across her pale skull. Head lice. I pluck one of the black specks and inspect the translucent edges of its torso before crushing it between my nails. Unphased, Milly keeps talking.

'My mum died two years ago when I was five. Max was eight, so he says that I can't even really remember her properly, that only he can, but I can, too. She was the most beautiful woman on the island. Everyone thought so. That's why my Dad got into so many fights at the pub. Now, he doesn't get in fights, but he still goes to the pub. That's where he takes all the money. Sometimes, he comes home with bags of coins, and he is in a really good mood, and we can eat ice cream for dinner. And, sometimes, he doesn't...'

Her voice trails off, and I don't press her to tell me what happens on those nights. The air gets cooler as the stars come out, and I pull my own wet hair into a bun, impulsively itching at my scalp.

'Where is your dad now?'

I am eager to go home and douse my head in eucalyptus oil but know that I can't leave her out at night by herself.

'He went to the shop to get some smokes. He said he'd be back soon. He doesn't like to talk to mum.'

I wrestle with the braid, but the knots are so thick that they stick out in uneven lumps.

'Maybe we should go find him?'

'No!' Milly shouts. 'No! I'm staying here.'

'Ok,' I soothe. 'Let's finish your hair first. I'm sure he'll be back soon.'

I pull more woolly orange strands into each section and continue weaving down her delicate back. Freckles smudge the skin on her neck.

'Are you here visiting your dad?' Milly asks.

'No,' I shake my head. 'My dad…'

'Oi!'

I am cut off by a deep voice bellowing behind us and the sound of heavy boots crunching the fallen leaves.

'Who the fuck are you?'

I stand up hurriedly and turn to face the man. Milly's father is as tall and hearty as an iron bark. He towers a foot over me.

My voice is weak and shrill. 'Hi, I'm Wallace.'

His eyes are sunk deep beneath thick brows. He grabs Milly firmly by the wrist and tugs her behind him.

'Owwwwww!'

'What are you doing with my daughter?'

'Nothing,' I stammer.

His eyes linger on my face, then his lips turn up in a callous smirk. He has the same features as Max.

'Ahhh, so you're that Jap bitch that my boy was telling me about.'

Blood rushes to the surface of my skin at the insult, but my words sink deep down into my gut. He waits for me to retort, but I can't.

'What? Forgot how to speak English?'

I want to be strong, but I almost whisper the only thing that comes into my mind.

'Actually, I was born here.'

'Stop it!' Milly wrestles against his grip. 'Wallace is my friend!'

'No, she isn't,' the man scoffs. 'She's a fucking slant. Your grandpop fought a war to keep people like her out. Go to the car.'

Milly hesitates.

'Now!'

She steps away cautiously.

Tears prick my eyes, but the man backs off, disappointed that I won't take his bait. He can see that he is fighting a lame animal.

'Just stay away from my kids,' he spits, and turns, pushing Milly in front of him.

She looks back at me, and I can tell by the way that her mouth is open wide that she is yelling, but I can't hear her.

My heart thuds in my ears.

6

I don't think Sandy Beach could ever be considered a real beach. It has no horizon and the bank on the other side looks close enough that I could swim to it. Sometimes, while I'm doing my counts, I think about going across, but even when the heat is unbearable and the water is cool and inviting, I never wade out further than my knees. On this side of the island the water is clearer than on the side where ferry comes, but it still has an ominous tinge. The currents stir the sand up so you can't see the bottom, and I imagine all sorts of creatures, ready to bite or sting me.

When I find the skinny bird lingering in the shrubs, it moves forward with purposeful steps. Its eyes lock onto mine and there's no doubt left in me. I just know that it's my father. We stand close to each other for a while, and then words start to fall out of my mouth.

'But why are men so confusing? I thought he was interested, then he completely shut me out. Then! When I saw him at the supermarket, it was like nothing ever happened. I could have died when Oji invited him to Christmas lunch. I hope it's not too weird that I'm talking to you about this.'

The fine feathers on the bird's head are like sleek hair combed back. He adjusts his neck from left to right to get a better look at me.

'There really isn't anyone else I can talk to. And this is supposed to be what girls talk to their fathers about. Right?'

Long clawed talons dig into the earth. He blinks and then probes the ground a few times with his long beak.

'I know you can't reply, but maybe we need to come up with some kind of code. Something like one peck for yes, two for no?'

He blinks again but doesn't pierce the earth this time.

'It's okay. We don't even really need to talk. We can just stay here a while.'

We look out towards the other side. It's more or less a mirror image of this side. A thin bank with florets of trees. At first, it looks like the island is wrapping around on itself like a snake curling and contracting its tail, but then I remember what Peter told me – that it's actually the inner coastline of North Stradbroke. Beyond the trees, there must be a real white beach that has its own sand and looks out to the real ocean beyond. For some reason, though, I'd prefer not to see it. It's enough to just know that it's there. At low tide, I think I could probably walk to the other side without getting my hair wet, but I don't do that either. Last week, Diego told me that they filmed *Jaws* on North Stradbroke, so the ocean over there is probably filled with sharks.

I take out the count table from my backpack and fill in the figures for today. Five birds, including my father. I am not sure whether I should include him in the count, but I do. I look back to him, and he looks so uncomfortable standing there, one angular leg bent at the knee. I wish he would just sit down, like a hen on its eggs.

Not wanting to go back yet, I take out my phone and see that there is another text message from my provider.

You have 13 new voicemails

'I suppose I should check my messages.'

He pecks the ground once.

'Ok,' I nod. 'You're the boss.'

Reluctantly, I dial the number.

'Hi Wallace. This is Robert Waters from Waters & Tate in Brisbane. We have been trying to reach you…'

I squeeze my eyes shut.

'Good morning, Wallace, It's Robert Waters again…'

'This is why I didn't want to check.'

'Good afternoon, Wallace, I am not sure if you are having problems with your phone. Are you getting my messages? We're still trying to reach you...'

'Wallace, Robert again...'

The same voice over and over. Both Sarah and my mother know better than to leave me voice messages. I delete them as I go.

'I suppose you want me to call him back, too?'

My father angles his head to see me clearly again, then pecks the ground.

'Wallace, It's Robert. Please give me a call when you can. We are eager to settle your father's affairs. Is there another lawyer or a family member you'd prefer us to speak to? Anyway, you've got my office number, and my personal mobile is...'

I scribble the number on the back of the count sheet.

'Not today,' I say.

The bird starts to walk slowly towards the hermit crabs that are now scurrying across the mud.

'You don't have to go yet.'

He eyes the tepid blue backs of the crabs, their tinny chorus intensifying as they try to move out of his path.

'Are you hungry?' I ask.

He probes the ground again but comes up with nothing. I think how magnificent it is, the way that those twig legs hold his torso up, and how his long beak doesn't dip down to the ground under its own weight, like those drinking bird toys you see in pubs sometimes, pecking away at the tip jar.

With a swift and purposeful movement, he scoops his head again, and this time emerges with a fat crab in his beak.

'That's it!'

Startled, he turns his head sharply and gives me a sideways glance.

'Sorry.'

He flicks the crab back and forth. I don't know how he expects it to fit it down his narrow throat. Tossing his head, he throws the crab to the ground, and with rapid jabs, dismembers two of its limbs. Then, he picks the round form up again, and draws figures of eight with his neck, positioning it symmetrically. Opening his mouth wider, he tilts his head, forcing the motionless crab backwards until almost inexplicably, it disappears into the gulf of his gullet.

'Well done!'

He looks at me once more, before turning and stalking towards the water, where the other birds stand.

Happiness washes over me.

While researching the birds I read that the Eastern Curlew is *Numenius* because their long and curved bills resemble the new crescent moon. The second part of their name is *Madagascariensis* because Mathurin-Jacques Brisson, and later Carl Linnaeus, wrongly attributed the first specimens to the Indian Ocean island 6000 kilometres outside of their actual range. A clerical error that stays with the species still. For the curlew, home is everywhere, even those places it has never touched down.

Watching the curlews, I know that it is not too long until they leave for their long migration. Travelling along coastlines, day and night, swimming their own long laps across the sky. Seeing my father among the other curlews, I feel sad, but I remember what Oji said about him always feeling more at ease with birds than people. I hope that it's true. Wherever he goes, I hope he feels at ease.

The surface of the shallow water trembles in concentric rings. Two curlews pace ankle deep, probing the circles for food. I wonder what prey awaits them below the water, miniscule yet seismic, and whether it has any inkling about the outwards painting of its whereabouts, or if it is fast enough to flee its own radiating betrayals.

My father looks back at me, but the other birds don't seem to notice I am there at all.

I stay until the light renders them sticks.

Kate's house is on the other side of the island to Oji's.

I ask Oji if I can borrow his car, and he just smiles and fetches the keys from the hook near the front door without making any comment about the fact that I don't have a license. The taste of new freedom is thrilling as I carefully round the corners, bumping prudently along the unsealed roads. The Honda is an automatic, so it's much easier to drive than Diego's car.

Kate's is a small brick construction tucked into a sloping hill, looking west towards Redland Bay. In her living room, prayer flags run along the awnings. There is a statue of a rotund four-faced Buddha on a small table under the front window. A large poster of the kabbalah tree-of-life is stuck to the wall with long slabs of yellowing sticky tape. An undiscerning, cosmopolitan spirituality adorns every available surface.

'Thanks for coming,' Kate says. 'Laura will be here soon.'

She goes into the kitchen and puts the kettle on. 'Peppermint or chamomile?'

I sit down on the pink velvet sofa. I wish coffee was an option but seeing as it isn't, I chose the least fragrant of the two. 'Chamomile, please.'

The front door sounds and a woman in her late twenties comes down the hallway. She is wearing Blundstone boots, skinny blue jeans, and a black long sleeve shirt. Laura is younger than I expected, plain but pretty. Her mousy hair is cut in a neat shoulder length bob.

'Hi,' she smiles.

Kate appears with three cups of tea, and we sit around the coffee table.

Laura opens a notebook and writes the date in the margin. 'Thanks for helping us. Between work and painting, I don't have much time. And neither does Kate.'

Kate takes an elastic from her hair and shakes her purple curls loose. 'Well, I have a little bit of time, but I am shocking when it comes to organising. Hard to believe I run a business, I know.'

'No problem,' I say. 'We should probably start with a venue?'

'I thought we could use the courtyard at the café.'

Laura writes courtyard – café in perfect cursive.

'Sure, and what about a date?'

Laura turns the pages of her book to a calendar and runs her pen along the lines. 'Probably good to get Christmas out of the way first. How about mid-January?'

'Will you still be here in January, Wallace?'

I shrug. 'Yeah, probably... Yes.'

I still haven't decided when I will go back to Sydney, and I'd be relieved to have a reason to stay into the new year. We talk for another half an hour or so, dividing tasks – like who will make the flyers, and who will organise the decorations – interspersed with general island gossip.

'Did you hear there was a protest against the marriage vote results on Macleay?'

Laura sneers. 'No way.'

'Yeah. That troll Robert something-or-other was behind it.'

'The one who owns the real estate agency?'

Kate nods. 'The one and only.'

'Figures. I heard his wife left him for another woman. That saucy permaculturalist.'

I laugh, sipping my tea. They seem to have a dynamic like Sarah's and mine, but without any of the extra complications. I am envious.

Laura sketches a courtyard with trellises and vines into her book.

'Fairy lights always look good at night,' I suggest.

She closes her eyes and sighs. 'Magical.'

There is something ethereal about Laura, yet there's a hint of sardonic wit in the upturned corner of her lips that suggests she isn't as timid as she looks. I like her right away.

We are interrupted by another set of footsteps tapping down the hallway.

'That must be the others,' Kate stands. 'Sorry, Wallace, I forgot to tell you. We have a bit of a group that meets on Wednesday afternoons. I lost track of time.'

I drink the last mouthful of my tea. 'Okay. That's okay. I can go.'

'No, no,' Kate insists. 'Why don't you join us?'

'Yes,' Laura agrees. 'Stay. Please.'

I have no idea what I would be staying for and, before I can ask, three more women enter the room. Amidst the greetings, I am forgotten, and I feel too awkward to leave or probe for an explanation.

Kate goes over to the bookcase, collects a stack of photocopied sheets, and hands one to each of us. She introduces me to the other women. Roberta, Christina, Julie. I smile and shake each of their hands. No one asks who I am or where I have come from. It seems to be taken for granted that I am just where I am supposed to be.

'We're going to do number one today.'

The instructions are printed on thin recycled paper. I read Pauline Oliveros' words slowly trying to make sense of what is going on.

I.

TEACH YOURSELF TO FLY

ANY NUMBER OF PERSONS SIT IN A CIRCLE FACING THE CENTER. ILLUMINATE THE SPACE WITH DIM BLUE LIGHT. BEGIN BY SIMPLY OBSERVING YOUR OWN BREATHING. ALWAYS BE AN OBSERVER. GRADUALLY ALLOW YOUR BREATHING TO BECOME AUDIBLE. THEN GRADUALLY INTRODUCE YOUR VOICE. ALLOW YOUR VOCAL CORDS TO VIBRATE IN ANY MODE WHICH

OCCURS NATURALLY. ALLOW THE INTENSITY TO INCREASE VERY SLOWLY. CONTINUE AS LONG AS POSSIBLE NATURALLY, AND UNTIL ALL OTHERS ARE QUIET, ALWAYS OBSERVING YOUR OWN BREATH CYCLE.

VARIATION: TRANSLATE VOICE TO AN INSTRUMENT.

Kate goes into another room further down the hallway and, soon after, the smell of burning patchouli wafts out. Scanning the words again, I look around to see if I can catch the eyes of the other women, to see if they are seriously going to do this. I start searching my mind frantically for an excuse to leave. Perhaps Oji might need help with the…

'Pauline was a bit of a revolutionary in the late sixties,' Laura explains with a smirk, as though she can sense my unease. 'An experimental musician from San Francisco. She wrote these sonic meditations as a means for expanding consciousness and healing. We started doing them as a bit of fun after Roberta bought them to our book club, but it turns out we all really enjoyed them. Your dad did, too. There is something nice about a bunch of people sitting in a room, connecting at a point beyond words. Deeper. You know? It's like we all travel to the centre of being together.'

'My dad came to these?'

Laura nods. 'Yes, he was a regular. The group isn't exclusively for women, it just mostly works out that way.'

Roberta, Christina and Julie take off their shoes and line them up against the wall. Now I can't leave. I have to find out what my father did here with these women. I take off my boots and place them next to the others.

The den doesn't have any furniture – only an assortment of large cushions and throw rugs scattered around the room. I choose a cushion that has the same design as the ones in my favourite vegetarian restaurant in Newtown; yellow tasseled with small reflective circles woven into the tapestry. I take a seat across from Kate, and Laura sits down directly next to her. Roberta, the older woman, sits cross-legged beside me and exhales deeply. Christina and Julie fill the circle and close their eyes, shoulders dropping forward, breasts resting on their bellies. They have soft, motherly shapes, and I know if I see them again I will struggle to recall who is who. The collective breathing in the room rises to an audible groan, something like the last warbled moments of a pigeon's coo, or a curlew's cry.

Discreetly, I look at the other women cast in blue light by a table lamp covered in a sheer scarf. They look like projections, almost translucent. I hope the scarf doesn't catch fire. I wonder what I am doing chanting in a dark room in the middle of the afternoon. I wonder what my father, a scientist, made of all this; but then I remember that he also liked to read poetry, and I start to realise that my father might have been very different to how I imagined him.

Is this how he learned to fly?

It is so rare to see faces free from expression, so I carefully inspect the slack lips and resting brows of the other women. The sound of breathing increases and reverberates off the walls. I feel a tremor in the pit of my stomach. Eventually, I give in and close my eyes. My breath starts to take shape as my exhalations fall into sync. A sound rises in my throat and passes through my lips with a gentle tickle. Once mixed with the chorus I can't tell which of the sounds is mine. The collective tone is peaceful, soothing. I feel warm and airy, on the edge of a dream.

After a while, the blue glow in the room seems to increase in intensity so that iridescent feathers of light are cast through my eyelids. I can no longer feel the rough thread of the cushion beneath my bare thighs, but I don't dare open my eyes or look down.

Underneath the house is a concrete slab with a small bricked off section in the right-hand corner. Oji likes to say that the closet-sized space is the laundry, but there is a hole where a window should be that opens to the outside, and when it rains water streams in leaving a large puddle around the base of the washing machine. It doesn't really resemble a laundry at all, and I am pretty sure it's completely unsafe.

I suggested that maybe we should combine the laundry with the bathroom upstairs, but Oji insists we can fix it.

'I think whoever owned the house before us planned to turn this into a self-contained level. A second bathroom, a living area, a bedroom. But they never got around to finishing it.'

There is a smashed toilet at the rear next to a half-finished shower stall.

'Not quite,' I raise my eyebrows at the washing machine propped up on wooden slats, attached to two rusted taps over a small metal sink. 'But at least they did the plumbing.'

'Yes, and we can tidy it up. Put a window in. Paint. Lay the tiles.'

'I admire your ability to see the best in a room.'

Oji chuckles and moves over to the washing machine, unscrewing the taps. I take hold of the other side, and we shimmy the heavy weight out into the empty space. It narrowly fits through the doorway.

Oji picks up a sledgehammer from the pile of tools spread over the concrete. 'Now, for the fun part.'

He goes back into laundry and with a groan, swings the hammer at the white tiles. A loud and pleasing crack rings out.

Oji beams and shakes his shoulders in delight. 'Your turn.'

He hands me the sledgehammer and steps back. I steady myself next to the wall, swinging the long wooden handle at chest height, connecting the metal head with force. Thwack. Shards of porcelain clink across the floor.

'That feels so good.'

'Again!'

Oji presses his palms over his ears as I take another swing, harder this time. Clackkkk. A whole section of tiles falls away.

Oji goes out and gets a crowbar, then sidles by me to pry away some loose pieces.

I grab the dustpan and crouch down to scoop broken tiles into a garbage bag, craning my neck to look up at Oji. He has started sweating and wipes his brow with the back of his arm.

'Did you know that he was meditating?'

Oji grunts as he struggles with a persistent square. 'Who?'

'My father.'

He stops for a moment and takes a swig of water, catching his breath.

'Oh yes. Yes. Aki was quite a spiritual man.'

'What do you mean? He was a scientist.'

Oji gestures for me to move out of the way and picks up the hammer again. I scurry backwards and shield my eyes. Krrrack.

He lowers the hammer. 'The two are not always mutually exclusive, you know.'

'Yeah, I guess not.'

I crouch again and scoop up the new debris.

Oji moves along the back wall and starts to maneuver the broken toilet. I grab the other side, and we bend and lift in unison – I awkwardly step backwards as Oji cradles the base and follows. We place it down next to the washing machine. I start to wonder how many sides of my father there were. Maybe he was like the many-faced Buddha at Kate's place that shifted as I walked around the room.

'What makes you say he was spiritual?'

Oji dusts his palms together then leans against the wall. 'I don't know. The way he talked about life. The books he was reading. Actually, one of the last conversations we had was quite spiritual, you could say.'

'Oh?'

I sit down on the stack of tiles.

'Yes. While he was sick, Aki immersed himself in a book called the Kojiki. It's one of the main texts of the Shinto religion.

He was fixated on one particular story about a young prince named Yamato Takeru.'

Listening to Oji, I stand up and start to unwrap the tiles. I hope that he will be cajoled into talking more by the promise of continued work. He eyes the tiles and grabs a broom, conceding.

'I don't remember the whole story, but some of it stuck with me,' his words interspersed with the swooshing of the broom against the concrete. 'Yamato Takeru was also known as Yamato Brave. Though I am not sure how brave he really was. He was vicious – bloodthirsty even. He was sent to battle by his Emperor father for killing his older brother.'

Oji pauses to collect a pile of dirt with the dustpan. When he rights himself, he continues. 'Yamato was a capable and cunning warrior. I remember that he disguised himself as a woman by dressing in his aunt's clothes to infiltrate enemy camps. And he used magical talismans to fight beasts and sea gods. The part that your father was most interested in was when Yamato met a mountain god in the form of a boar. He grew very tired and said something like: within my heart, I have always felt as though I might soar like a bird, but now my legs will not walk, they are swollen and bowed. Aki said he related to that sentiment deeply. It was in the days when he could barely get himself out of bed.'

Oji's eyes turn glassy as he recalls this image of my father. Until now, I hadn't given much consideration to his illness, or how bad his condition was. Oji has never spoken about it in detail, and I hadn't thought of him as bedridden, frail. This new information strikes me as overwhelmingly sad. Was Oji caring for my father? Cooking his meals? Bathing him? Was he so sick that he had to vomit into a bucket by the bed? Was the smell of his ailing body so strong that all the windows had to be opened?

Before I can think of a way to ask Oji any of these questions, he presses on. 'Then, Yamato continued to get weaker as he crossed the land, but rather than succumbing to a conventional death, he transformed into a great white bird.'

I stop arranging the tiles and look up at Oji in shock. I search his eyes for a hint that he might know about my father's transformation, but he turns away. Maybe the *Kojiki* held the secrets that allowed him to shift forms. Maybe that's where he got the idea. The image of the warrior's robes morphing into spreading wings against a backdrop of mountains fills the empty air in the room.

'So, I guess, that's what he wanted too. I guess that's why he...'

Oji clears his throat but doesn't respond, just nods his head. It is all the confirmation that I need. I step closer and touch his arm. Buoyed by my touch, Oji keeps speaking, as though reaching a conclusion might rid him of the upsetting memories of his last days with my father.

'There was one line in the story that Aki kept repeating to himself over and over.'

'What was it?'

Oji closes his eyes recalling the words. 'At the breakfast table, in his study sipping whiskey, in bed with the book resting on his chest. The beach plover crosses not the land, but rather the rocks.'

'Hm,' I let the strange phrase circle in my mind. 'What do you think it means?'

'I don't know. I asked him about it a few times, and he said he wasn't sure either. He thought it might have been something to do with the beach plover, like the curlew, existing in a place between two worlds. Not quite a creature of the land, but not one of the sea, either. In Yamato's case, he was not quite part of the living world anymore, but not yet in the land of the dead.'

I try to process the cryptic story and know that it contains so much more than I can grasp in this moment.

'How does the story end?'

Oji sighs. 'Well, Yamato Takeru soars towards the heavens and flies away. To I don't know where. I don't know which world.'

I picture the great bird lifting up above the mudflats. A band of small children run bare-footed below trying to keep up with the speed of its mighty wing strokes. Quickly, they fall behind. Small legs putter and stop. Short of breath, the children stand craning their necks towards the sky. Forearms lay across their brows to shield from the sun.

The bird flies further and further up, edges diffusing, and soon, the brilliant flood of unfiltered light absorbs its entire shape.

7

Indigo petals sit up like fine crystal bowls.
I still haven't gotten used to the sight of potted weeds on the
back table, but I must admit, they are pretty. I give them a mist
of spray from the bottle that Oji bought to keep them strong. I
tried to tell him that they would probably survive without any
care at all, but he just shrugged.

'Better to be safe.'

Oji was sad to hear that Morning Glory is a pest here. He
told me that he fought my father for days about pulling the
bushes up from the back garden and refused to believe that they
would strangle the native plants.

'It looks almost exactly like Okinawa Morning Glory.'

When he first arrived, the plants were the only things
that reminded him of home. He missed Japanese flowers –
so different from our spiky waratahs and sunny wattles – but
settled for a compromise: one planter box that he tends to with
diligence. He hasn't seen to the box today, so I carefully collect
the fallen petals from the damp soil.

Inside, the front screen door opens and then clicks closed.

There are voices in the living room. Oji is speaking to a
woman. I didn't know we were expecting company. Come to
think of it, no women have visited the house since I arrived.
He is speaking English, so I know that it's not his ex-wife, and
I am sure he would have told me if an international guest was
coming. There would have been frantic cleaning, preparation of
linen, serious conversations about the menu. I gather the shed
petals in my palm and go inside to investigate.

Jill is standing in the doorway.

'Mum!'

'Surprise!'

She steps forward and throws her arms around my shoulders. Shocked, I slump into her breast and drop the wilted petals onto the floor. Her floral summer dress is soft against my cheek as I inhale her familiar scent: Chanel No. 5 mixed with a clean soapy musk. Straightening out, I hold her at arm's length: skin buffed and creamy, highlighted blonde hair hanging in loose curls. I wonder if she came directly from the salon and wouldn't put it past her to find one between the airport and the ferry terminal.

'What are you doing here?'

Jill's meticulously lined lips turn down in disappointment. 'I thought you might be happier to see me.'

'I am! I am!' I hug her again. 'I'm just surprised.'

Oji steps back tactfully and starts sorting the mail on the dining table.

'Did you already meet Oji?'

'I did. I know I probably should have called first, but I thought it would be a nice Christmas present. Plus, you're so hard to get a hold of these days.'

Jill shifts her weight, and I note how beautiful my mother is – and not just because of her surface treatments. There is something about her presence that changes a room.

I gesture to the plush blue sofa. 'Come in, sit down!'

'No, no,' Jill shakes her head. 'There's a motel down the road. I don't know what it's like, but I am sure it'll be fine. I'll stay there. I just thought I would pop in first to tell you I'm here. I don't want to be any inconvenience…'

I've seen that motel. I am pretty sure it's deserted. I haven't seen a single person or car there even though it's almost Christmas and school holidays are already in full swing.

I shake my head. 'I'm sure you can stay here, right Oji?'

He looks up, his vacant expression cracking into a smile. 'Of course, of course.'

'You can take my room, and we can set up the air mattress in the study.'

Oji grimaces at this suggestion.

'What?' I ask. 'Is that okay?'

'Sure, sure,' he says. 'That mattress just isn't very comfortable. Make sure to use an underlay.'

I nod, but I can sense that there is something else that Oji isn't saying.

'No, really…' Jill objects halfheartedly but is already pulling her suitcase into the house.

I push the bag against the wall and grab her hand. 'Let me show you around!'

'So, this is what you've been up to.'

She surveys the space with her senses, craning her neck to look at every corner, rubbing her hands along the furniture, sniffing the air. I conduct a tour, vividly describing the before and after.

'This was slime-green lino before we put the floating floorboards down.'

I point out the cracked plywood cabinets, now transformed into shiny melamine nooks and crannies that open when pushed, revealing stainless steel appliances. 'Pretty impressive, right?'

I touch the right-hand edge of the cabinet above the stove, and it pops open to show an assortment of spices.

'You have been busy! But then I suppose you have been here for almost two months now.'

I can tell that she isn't that impressed.

'We both have.'

'Yes, indeed,' Oji adds. 'It would have taken forever if I was working by myself.'

'I guess it's one way to spend your time. Personally, I'd hire the professionals. I'm just terrible at anything handy. And I thought my daughter was, too, but there you go!' Jill laughs coarsely.

I collect her heavy metallic suitcase and wheel it down the hallway. 'I'll show you your room.'

Peripherally, I see Oji crouch and pick the discarded petals up off the floor, dusting the dirt away with his spare hand.

Jill follows behind with an oversized handbag.

'You do know Christmas is only a week away?'

She shrugs. 'I haven't been to Queensland since my twenties. I didn't know what the weather would be like.'

'Please don't tell me you bought a winter coat?'

'No, but I did bring my Ugg boots.'

Her high heels give hollow clicks against the laminate floors as I deposit the suitcase just inside the door of the bedroom.

'The bed is a bit old, but it's pretty comfortable. I hope it's okay.'

I think of how my role has changed. Now I am the one offering up the guest room. Compared to when I arrived, the walls are the colour of slate, and the ceiling has a fresh coat of white paint covering the watermarks. The bed is made with a thick waffled bedspread, powder blue cushions, and a charcoal throw rug. Apart from a few boxes still stacked in the corner, it looks like a country bed and breakfast.

Jill crinkles her nose. 'Cosy. Cute.'

'Why don't you settle in, and I'll go find the air mattress.'

I give my mother's hand a squeeze, and she nods. Despite the surprise, I am glad to see Jill. I realise that I have missed her – the terrible jokes, the discussions about bad reality TV – everything. Down the hall in the linen cupboard, I find the plastic mattress on the top shelf, tucked away next to the electric heater. When I return, Jill is still standing in the doorway, as though she needs an invitation for every movement in this house.

'Everything okay?'

She jumps – she has been travelling with her thoughts and my words have pulled her back.

'Yes, yes,' she nods. 'I'm fine.'

She steps into the room, kissing her palm and blowing the last traces of her secret musings in my direction. I can't quite catch them.

My fist closes around empty air.

In the week before Christmas, the IGA gets special deliveries every day, so the tubs and shelves are overflowing with fresh produce and themed cartons. Oji counts the potatoes for the potato salad.

'I'll get some eggs,' I say.

Jill has already disappeared to try and find the shampoo she likes, because amidst her spontaneous decision to come, she left hers back in Sydney. Oji and I push the trolley around families jostling for the last boxes of Christmas crackers.

'Don't worry, I already got some of those.'

I turn towards the voice behind us and see that Diego is holding a box of lolly-wrapped bonbons. The smiling faces of reindeers fringed in bells and tinsel beam at me. Looking at Diego's mop of hair falling over his eyes, I understand the concept of island fever more than ever. I feel claustrophobic – boxed in by the heavy bars of fluorescent light.

Oji claps his hands. 'Good man!'

'Do I need to bring anything else?'

'Just yourself.'

I look for Jill among the crowd. A few feet away a little boy bursts a bag of candy canes that release an intoxicating minty vapor as they spill across the floor under the trample of bustling feet.

'How are you?' Diego asks.

'Good, good,' I smile, but I'm distracted.

Jill appears in front of the commotion and steps daintily around the crushed sugar. 'There you are! This place is a riot. Looks like I'll be slumming it with Pantene.'

Diego looks on, unable to make the connection.

'Diego, this is my mum, Jill.'

Jill turns to face him and reaches out a manicured hand. 'Oh goodness! How embarrassing! Nice to meet you.'

He takes her hand obligingly. 'Likewise.'

I wait for Diego to insert the standard lines that men offer about us being adopted sisters or cousins, but he doesn't. Instead, he keeps eye contact with me and gives me a bemused grin.

Throughout my life men have been unable to look directly at my mother. It's as though her glow momentarily blinds them. In Year 5, my teacher, Mr. Oakley, spent the best part of a year bumbling and fumbling in her presence. He called a parent-teacher interview just to tell Jill how intelligent I was but spent most of the time organising the stationary on his desk. He was the first male teacher I had, and he was nothing like my Year 4 teacher Mrs. Hembrow who came to meetings with a neatly handwritten list of conversation points, so I wondered if maybe all men were endearingly incompetent. Eventually, over the summer break, Mr. Oakley married Lillian Baker's mother.

Jill smirked when the news got passed down the gossip line. 'It was only a matter of time.'

A moderately attractive, educated man, among all those single mothers – and he already showed an interest in their children. He was sitting prey, but to my disappointment, my mother wasn't hungry.

I had spent many nights wondering what it would be like to have Mr. Oakley as a father. He was good at sports, told funny jokes, and almost never raised his voice. As I lay awake, imaginary footballs came flying at me, and I caught them gracefully. The world looked different atop a man's shoulders. Then, my paternal dreams were tossed with poise from Lillian Baker's flower girl basket. We didn't get invited to the wedding – I don't think any of the other students' families did because the whole affair was a little bit scandalous – and the next year the new family moved to another city, so I never saw any of them again.

Standing before us, Diego doesn't shift his weight like Mr. Oakley did but looks at his watch as though he has somewhere else to be.

'Diego will be joining us at Christmas,' Oji says.

'Fabulous!' Jill beams, 'The more the merrier.'

A frazzled teenage attendant appears next to the candy cane debris with a broom and tries to set up a hazard sign. He politely asks a woman to move her trolley, and she almost rams it into him as she pushes on towards the legs of ham. Candied gems are kicked under the aisles to join a whole assortment of rotting treasures that lay just out of sight.

I feel anxious. This is the biggest crowd I have seen in one place since I arrived on the island. I don't even dare to think about how busy the Pitt Street Mall is at this very moment.

'Let's get out of here,' I say to Oji.

'Yes, there's still plenty to do at home.'

'I'll see you soon, Wally.'

Diego makes one last attempt at cordiality, and I muster a smile.

With a two-fingered wave, he disappears towards the perilous tower of fruitcake as Jill casts exaggerated looks back and forth. When he is out of sight, she pokes me in the ribs.

'Ouch!'

'Who was that?'

'Just a friend.'

'A very good-looking friend.'

She pokes me again, but I don't say anything more – I just listen to the steady beep of the cash register ringing us closer and closer to the end of another year.

Honey tempeh and green vegetables simmer in big stone bowls.

'You really cooked this?' Jill asks me.

I nod, 'Oji taught me.'

'It's delightful. Well-done.'

She holds a sliver of tempeh dripping with golden sauce up to the light, inspecting it for any giveaway that it might actually come from the Chinese restaurant, even though I already explained to her that it's never open.

Jill's first days on the island pass easily enough, but, for me, the hours are long. I wake at six and wait for her to get up so that she won't wonder about where the food and crockery are kept or how to work the new coffee machine. When she finally rises at nine or ten, she potters about getting ready for an hour, as though she has a full schedule of important meetings. Next, she eats a bowl of fruit salad then reads her phone for most of the day. Occasionally, she'll switch to the latest Kathy Reichs novel for a chapter or two, before making a coffee, and returning to YouTube and online tabloids. Apart from the trip to the supermarket, we don't leave the house. This morning, when I asked her if she wanted to do something today, she just shrugged her shoulders.

'Is there anything to do here? Plus, remember, I'm on holidays. I'm relaxing.'

She put her Ugg boots up on the coffee table and reclined further, giving me a wink. We settled for watching a movie while Oji finished erecting the gazebo in the back yard so that it would be ready in time for Christmas lunch.

'I can't believe the Internet isn't fast enough to stream something!'

Jill slowly sorted through the small stack of DVDs on the bookshelf, settling for a romantic comedy. As we laughed and teared up at all the same moments, I watched my mother closely. I have always struggled to see a resemblance when I look in the mirror – perhaps only the slightest hint of her upturned nose, or a certain sharpness to the collarbones – but watching the film, I noticed how we reflected in our mannerisms. We both leaned our heads against a clenched fist with our legs tucked under our laps, and we both propped forwards when the male suitor said something particularly coy.

'Why on earth did your father own this movie?'

'Maybe he had a soft spot for Renee Zellweger. She does look a little bit like you.'

I held the cover next to Jill's face. She opened her mouth in mock offence and threw a cushion at me.

'Wash your mouth out!'

I launched at her, wrapping my arms around her waist in a playful hug as she tickled my ribs – our laughter trilling on the same register.

The dinner conversation is polite and constrained. Jill and Oji skirt around topics concerning my father. He is the link that binds them, but their impressions of him are so vastly dispersed across time and space, I suppose they fear that they might impact on the other's memories with some unwanted or unknown piece information.

'So, you're working as an Environmental Consultant now? What does that mean?'

'Well, I spend all my time behind a desk. I lead a team that does environmental assessments for major developments. It's not exactly what I imagined when I was a student. It's a lot of work, but the money is very good. Any developers nosing around here? What are the property prices like on the island?'

'Cheap as chips, as they say. Agents like to promise that we are on the verge of a boom, but, realistically, I don't think there will be a rise any time soon. Unless they build that bridge that they have been talking about for decades. No major developments that I know of. And besides, there is a bit of a problem with unemployment, and methamphetamines.'

Jill shoots me a look of horror. 'Ice?'

'It's not that bad,' I assure her. 'Some of the houses look a bit dodgy, and the people are a bit rough around the edges, but everyone keeps to themselves. Honestly, we barely see anyone else.'

Oji sits at the head of the table, and I sit across from my mother. The cheap IKEA dining table is doll's furniture compared to the rustic acacia slab that easily seats twelve in Jill's apartment.

'So, I was thinking we could spend Christmas here with Oji, then we can fly back together on Boxing Day, or the day after.'

Oji shifts uncomfortably in his seat, and I can see that he doesn't want me to go. The sharp pang in my stomach tells me that I'm not ready to leave either. Plus, there is Laura's exhibition, but I don't want to bring that up with my mother yet.

'Maybe,' I say non-committedly.

Jill's eyes widen in frustration, but when she opens her mouth to say something else, Oji interjects with, 'has Wallace told you about the bird work she has been doing?'

Jill pauses, a fork loaded with broccoli in front of her mouth. 'No, she's never shown any interest in ecology.'

'Yes, turns out she is quite good at it, too, so Peter tells me.'

'Peter Kenney! That old codger is still going?'

Oji nods his head. 'You know him?'

'Yes, we did quite a few surveys with him back in the day.'

I imagine Jill and my father with Peter. I imagine a time when they were a we. I can see my mother carrying her own equipment, refusing to let the men do anything for her. Keeping up with Peter's quips. Hanging on my father's words as he spoke knowledgeably about the different species gathered in the estuary.

'I'm not really any good,' I grimace. 'It's just carrying things really. Helping to finish what Dad started.'

My hand freezes. The word leaves a strange taste in my

mouth. I have never addressed my father that way before. Jill is shocked too.

'So, Dad now, is it?'

I look down into my wineglass.

'He was never your dad when he was here. He took off once, and now he's gone for good. I'd love to know what he's done to earn the title.'

My eyes sting, and a knot forms in the back of my throat. 'Nothing,' I murmur. 'I didn't even mean to say it. It was just a slip of the tongue.'

'Right,' Jill nods, but seeing that I am upset, doesn't press further.

I swallow deeply and pick at my food.

After a few moments, Jill sighs and mutters. 'Sorry, Wallace. It was just a surprise to hear you call him that. I know this has been... hard.' She takes another sip of her wine. 'Your father was a very gifted ecologist. I'm sure he would be very happy that you're working with Peter.'

'Yes, most definitely,' Oji agrees, pleased at this turn in the conversation. 'He really loved his work.'

'That's probably why he'll make such a good bird,' I add.

Oji and Jill exchange looks. Jill laughs nervously.

'What do you mean?'

'Well, I saw him,' I look to Oji for reassurance. 'When I was with Peter. It wasn't really an accident, was it Oji? I am sure he meant to become a curlew.'

My mother's jaw goes slack. She looks as though she is about to ask another question, but Oji holds up the bottle of wine to stop her.

'More?'

We nod in unison. I am grateful to Oji. I don't feel like explaining about the skinny bird to my mother. I don't want to have to share him with anyone else.

Pouring the remainder of the wine into our glasses, Oji stands and puts the empty bottle into the recycling bin.

'Do you think we should do fruit cake or apple pie for dessert at Christmas?'

I grin. 'How about both?'

'Why didn't I think of that?'

Jill nods distractedly, but her thoughts are elsewhere. She gives a strained smile.

Discreet jazz plays from the portable CD player on the kitchen bench – a subdued melody of piano and spangled chimes.

We finish the meal in silence.

Jill appears in the doorway of the study.

I am already tucked under a rough tartan rug, the air mattress hugging my sides. She sits on the end of the bed, and it sinks under her weight with a toot. We laugh.

'It's good to see you, to spend time with you again,' Jill says. 'You left so soon after your trip. It feels like it's been an age.'

'I know. It's good to see you, too.'

'I'm worried about you. You barely take any of my calls. It's easy in mourning for the world to seem very strange…'

I cut her off. 'I'm sorry. For being so absent. I just need to be here. It's hard to explain.'

'And I'm sorry for what I said before. It's just weird seeing you in this place. In this world. Without me. Have you thought about talking to someone else about all this? A counselor?'

'No, I don't need a counselor. I just need to be here.'

'Okay. I know you're looking for your own answers. But I just wish I could help. You know, I spoke to Oji, your father's accident, it was…'

I wriggle down and rest my head on Jill's knee, cutting her off.

'Tell me a story.'

Jill laughs.

'Not too grown up for that yet?'

'Never.'

'I must admit it was nice hearing that you've been in the field. It reminded me of my first trips.'

When I was young, I lapped up Jill's stories about the animals she encountered during her early fieldwork in Malay Borneo. My head became a zoo populated with strange creatures. Dragging limbs, orange fur, and bulbous noses all combined to make forms that were not quite fantasy, not quite real.

'I'm not sure if I've told you this one,' Jill says, 'but, on one trip, when I was in the second summer of my Bachelor's degree, I was in Borneo for the first time. I would have been a little bit younger than you are now. And still very naïve. We were conducting a bio-diversity survey to aid in slowing down the deforestation in the area.'

I have heard the story before, but I don't stop her. I remember the first time Jill told it to me: I was thirteen, sitting on a stool at the kitchen bench in Grandma Sue's apartment before we sold it, scooping ice cream directly from the tub. My feet dangled above the floor, skimming the metal footrest as I swung my legs. Jill spoke about how everyone who visited the region where she was working wanted to snap a picture with the wide-eyed, long-limbed Slow Loris because of its ability to induce coos of adoration. Even Jill, who liked to think that she was above reducing wild animals to postcards, longed to see one up close.

Her voice is wistful. 'Each night, I went with three other students to try and find one. After dinner, we went out with our head torches and flashlights, scanning up and down the thick tree trunks hoping to catch a glimpse of amber fur. Some nights, we stayed out for hours getting scraped by branches and bitten by leeches, but, night after night, we returned to our hard bunk beds disappointed, scratching at the bites on our ankles until dawn.'

Jill recounts how, on the final night of the trip, after they had no luck in finding the animal themselves, the most determined male student in the group paid a local worker to help them. At first reluctant, the short Malay man took the bills and walked down with them just a few metres from the research centre. Reaching up, he pulled a soft mound from the bough of a tree, gripped it firmly by the neck, and held its body far away from his own. He knew about the toxic venom that the animal secreted from a gland in its armpit and coated along the combs of its teeth while it groomed itself. Distressed, it emitted a foul smell, hung limp, and blinked its dinner plate eyes.

While the burgeoning ecologists snapped their pictures, Jill said she felt guilty posing next to the furry body stiff with terror, but she tells me that she still looks back at the photograph from time to time, knowing that one day in the not-so-distant future, when the Slow Loris is gone, she will be glad to have the memento. Maybe someday she will show it to her grandchildren, regaling them with stories from that briefly held breath before extinction.

'Grandchildren!' I scoff.

Jill laughs, stroking my hair. 'A mother can dream.'

When I first heard the story, I felt like there was some moral that I was meant to glean from it that was lost on me. All I felt was an intense pride at Jill's adventurous spirit. It wasn't until a few years later when I was finishing high school that I remembered the story again.

On my graduation night, my mother asked if, now that I was becoming an adult, I wanted to make contact with my father. I thought about it for a long time, and while I knew that he was easily within reach – that I could click a few buttons and find his phone number or email address – I decided that I didn't want to shine my light on him and stare into his eyes. Like the local worker, who each night left the animal to its own devices, I had no desire to find that which did not wish to be found.

By the time I learned that my father had returned to Australia, I felt a little differently. I was only a few years younger than my mother had been when I was born, and I had more of an understanding about the immense responsibility that having a child would bring. The thought terrified me. I didn't begrudge the compulsion to flee.

Now, being here, in his house, on his island, it is like walking into a bedroom just after the inhabitant has left. Every object betrays his essence: a scent emitted from the clothes in the open drawers, the faded hint of a stranger's sweat, manliness hidden in the folds of the linen. I know it isn't Oji's smell, because his is supple and earthy. I have always been fascinated by the aromas of men. I remember how the first boy I kissed, Aaron Riley, wore his father's Old Spice to impress me. The pungent citrus was so different from anything in our feminine household. Even when he wasn't around, it stayed with me for a week.

Lying in my father's office, I inhale deeply and close my heavy eyelids.

'Get some rest,' Jill says. She leans down and kisses my forehead.

I am already crossing the threshold to sleep, traversing twenty metres up a wooden ladder nailed to the trunk of a towering tree. From the elevated vantage I look east out over the canopy as the sun is rising, watching thousands of seeds spin down through the misted blanket towards the ground. In her stories, Jill told me about the Dipterocarp trees that only spawn every seven years in perfect unison so that the whole sky is filled with woody spirals for days.

From the treetop platform, I survey the valley that Alfred Russel Wallace and his Malay assistants must have trekked through more than a century before my mother had. I wonder if much has changed in a hundred years across landscapes largely untouched by humans. Time is both compressed and elongated, eons and seconds in the same breath. Some large trees die and topple, creating new habitat for beetles, frogs and lizards. Otherwise, there is only a constant replenishing cycle. Flowers blooming and then falling away to give rise to new buds. Generations of animals passing through the same gullies.

I feel warm.

A rainforest of pitcher plants and orchids sprout around my sleepy body. My eyelids flutter and the ceiling is transformed into a humid expanse, opening up to soaring greenery. I take a deep breath of the honeyed air.

Winged seeds cover the whole vista, spinning down to my makeshift bed, like so many dancers fanning their skirts.

8

On Christmas day, the house is buzzing.
The humidity combined with the heat from the oven gives all the surfaces a damp glow. At midday it's already climbing above thirty degrees. Peter comes through the front door wearing a white singlet and khaki shorts cut above the knee, a carton of beer tucked under his arm. Turning to greet him, I burn my hand on a baking tray.

'Ouch!'

'You right, love?'

I nod, sucking my fingertip.

'Everyone is out back.'

Peter starts towards the fridge with a six-pack, but I hold my hands up in protest.

'No room! There's an esky in the yard.'

Peter nods.

I swing around on my heels to stir the gravy.

'Alright, busy bee, I'll leave you to it. Keep up the good work, though. It smells bloody great.'

I give a gracious smile and watch out the kitchen window as Peter approaches the table under the gazebo. It's the biggest Christmas I've ever had. Oji, Kate, Diego and Jill sit around sipping drinks and nibbling on chocolate-coated raisins. Peter is greeted warmly.

When I was young, Grandma Sue used to roast a chicken for Christmas and the three of us would take a picnic down to the park near the beach. In later years, my mother and I went to the video store and hired a stack of movies that we watched back-to-back while eating an eclectic array of junk food. It wasn't a traditional Christmas, but it was our tradition, and I liked it that way. The last few years, I'd spent the day with Sarah, rebelling against the familial aspects of Christmas entirely. I am not sure how this Christmas fits in.

I turn to check the roast vegetables again.

Oji appears at the back door. 'Leave that for a minute. It's never going to cook if you keep opening the oven.'

I hesitate, 'Okay, okay. I just don't want anything to burn.'

'Relax. Come and sit for a while.'

Giving in, I take a bottle of Sauvignon Blanc from the fridge and pour myself a glass.

Outside, Jill and Peter are deep in discussion about the old days.

'Sheryl Landers passed on a couple of years back. Never changed, though. She could still out drink any man on any field trip right 'til the end.'

'I remember when she got so blind on that whimbrel survey that she went into your tent by accident and passed out in your sleeping bag. The sound of your shriek when you came back from the loo and found her there!'

Jill cackles, eyes shining like decorative lights.

Oji and I didn't buy any Christmas lights – we didn't even buy a tree. Instead, I decked a fallen gum branch with seashells and dried flowers and propped it in the corner of the living room. When Oji saw it, he gave his signature seal of approval: a loud handclap, a nod, and a chuckle.

'You'd scream, too, if you found old Shez in your bed!'

Jill sprays a grape sweet glittering breath in Peter's direction. Covering her mouth, she laughs harder. She is already tipsy.

I take a seat next to Diego, and he sniffs the air approvingly. 'So, you're a better cook than you are a driver?'

'Hardly.' I hold up my scorched fingers. 'I have no idea what I'm doing in there. Oji is teaching me, but I've got more scars than skills.'

He laughs. 'Well, you're a good student at least.'

Jill looks over at Diego, girlishly tilting her head to the side.

'So, Diego, what do you eat in Colombia at Christmas time?'

'Ahhhh,' he sighs, 'I'd give anything for some buñuelos… they're these little balls of bread, kind of like donuts. Crunchy on the outside but soft and fluffy on the inside.'

He pulsates his tongue against the roof of his mouth. 'Mmmm, sounds delicious.'

'Then there is this custard to go with them called natilla.'

I roll my eyes and wonder if my mother is warming up for her reality TV audition. I interrupt the performance.

'What about in Japan, Oji? What do you eat for Christmas there?'

'Well, we don't really celebrate Christmas in the same way… but fried chicken, I suppose?'

'Fried chicken!' Kate exclaims.

The table erupts in laughter.

'You should have told me,' Peter teases. 'I could have ducked in and grabbed something from the Colonel on the way.'

Oji shrugs his shoulders and grins. 'Well, not me personally. I don't eat chicken, but it seems to be what the young people like.'

The oven timer goes off inside the house.

'Speaking of food…'

I scurry inside with Oji to serve up the spread of dishes. There is a whole baked fish marinated in lemon, thyme and garlic. I take the potato salad out of the fridge – the saffron egg yolks a splash of colour amidst the white. Oji pulls the roast pumpkin and carrots from the oven and sweet steam fills the kitchen. Through the window, I see Jill and Diego deep in conversation and drain a little hot water from the corncobs onto my fingers.

'Argh!'

'Careful,' Oji warns. 'You won't have any fingers left soon.'

I run cold water over my throbbing skin.

Jill laughs hysterically at something Diego says.

Back and forth, we ferry the trays outside, turning down offers of help. I take great pleasure in playing host with Oji. He places the fish at the centre of the table and everyone *oohs*. I wedge myself between Jill and Diego, positioning the vegetable trays. Oji unwraps the salads while I arrange the condiments and refill the glasses.

'Looks delicious; thanks for the invite,' Diego says.

'Me, too,' Kate chirps. 'It gets a bit lonely over here sometimes, and my parents don't really celebrate Christmas back home. They say it's too commercial, and I couldn't take another year of them ranting about the woes of capitalism after a couple of shandies.'

'Yeah, my kids are away with their families, and it's hard to keep up with the little ones at this time of year,' adds Peter. 'All those new toys to be assembled. All the shrieking.' He presses his temples in mock pain.

Jill gives a tight-lipped smile.

Oji bows his head. 'You're all very welcome. And thank you to Wallace for all her hard work.'

I lean in and give Oji a hug. 'Let's eat!'

The conversation is lively. Food is devoured. Wine flows.

'Did you see what they did with the sea wall at Saemangum? Thirty-three kilometres of wetland reclaimed, Aki was telling me...'

'Of course *Die Hard* is a Christmas movie! The best there is, I reckon.'

'Yeah, the safety on the job sites could be a lot better. But, if you don't want to do it, there's always some other poor migrant guy trying to support his family that will step in.'

'Oh, this old thing? I've had it for years.'

'Where did all the birds go?'

'What's an egg nog?'

'Next year... I'm not sure. Next year still seems so far away, funnily enough.'

'That one with the comedian guy playing the elf... I like that one, too.'

'I saw these beautiful Japanese tarot decks. I have only ever done readings for myself, but I could...'

'It seems like my friends from high school all have babies and husbands, or six figure salaries. But I don't even have a driver's license yet.'

'They say there used to be so many birds there, that, from a distance you could mistake them for clouds.'

'Have you seen that new show with the medium on cable? I was almost convinced until I read the *Women's Weekly* exposé.'

'Guitar, mostly, but I dabbled in bass, too. Could never keep a decent beat on the drums, though. What about you?'

'What about that old one, with the little girl from Matilda?'

'There was an internship at this boutique gallery, but, to be honest, I don't really like modern art that much.'

'I don't have a musical bone in my body.'

'No way, too corny for me. I need action or toilet humour.'

'This fish is to die for, Wallace, you will need to cook like this for me when we get home in a few days.'

Kate gives me a puzzled look. 'But the exhibition isn't until...'

'I'm not going home yet.'

'What?'

Jill's voice rises above the rest, and the table falls silent.

'Yes, you are. I already booked the flights. It's all...'

'I'm sorry, I should have said something earlier, but I'm staying.'

My voice is soft yet assured. I can see Jill is upset, but I'm so relieved to have said what I really want that I can't take it back. Jill opens her mouth to object again but instead takes the last gulp of her wine. Diego and Peter make eye contact and raise their eyebrows. Oji leans over to the portable CD player and turns up the volume. Mariah Carey's Christmas album picks up in tempo.

'I love this one.'

With the clap of Oji's hands, the tension in the air splinters. I turn to Jill and try to lighten the mood.

'Oh, my god. Do you remember how you used to play this every year as soon as it hit December?'

My mother doesn't say anything – just stands, picks up her empty plate and leaves the table.

Mariah's saccharine voice croons: 'All I want for Christmas is yoooouuuu…'

'I love this one, too!'

Peter stands up from his seat and starts toe tapping his way across the lawn pointing his fingers at the ground in sharp jabs while twisting his hips in an awkward jig. Oji joins in waving his hands from side to side around his waist. Kate starts her own interpretive dance, soaring her arms in long arcs. I cover my eyes and laugh. Diego pulls me to my feet and forces me into a strange salsa hybrid.

I look inside the house to where Jill is rinsing plates in the kitchen. I gesture for her to come back outside, but she just smiles and shakes her head.

Diego lifts my hand, readying me for a twirl.

'I don't know how to dance!'

'Is there anything you do know how to do?'

I look around at the discordant limbs flailing and jiving behind me and let my body fall into rhythm with the music; a sheen of sweat forms over my skin as I twist through the muggy afternoon.

The mood subdues with the colours of dusk.

By the time the sky is mauve, the guests have dispersed around the house. Full from dessert, Peter is having a nap in the study. Kate and Jill are reading in the living room with cups of tea, while Oji is filling the dishwasher with the second load. I go outside and find Diego sitting on a picnic blanket.

'I have something for you,' he says.

'No!' I exclaim. 'No presents! That's what Oji said on the invitation.'

'Well, that's too bad.'

I take the red wrapped oblong and peel back the paper to find a set of fluffy dice.

'For when you get your own car.'

'That might be a little while away yet,' I smile. 'But thank you.'

My mind races trying to think of what kind of gift I can conjure from inside the house, then I feel a hard shape in my jean pocket. I sit down next to Diego and hand him a banded tulip seashell that I found by the shore.

'It's not much,' I say, 'but it's beautiful. Maybe you can put it on your dashboard.'

Diego takes the shell and holds it up to inspect the peach interior. We both lean forward, trying to peer inside, but can only see the smooth alabaster walls of its domed tunnel scooping inward. Diego holds the opening to my ear – the faintest whisper of ocean.

'Thank you,' he says. 'It's a good one.'

I stretch my legs out on the rough tartan rug and lean back on my arms. The crescent moon reclines, too, cradling the full moon's shadow. Over the bush, the sky is dappled with stars. I think about how in some places the sky is always a busy luminous grey.

'There aren't stars like this in Sydney.'

'Or in Bogota.'

Our bodies are close again, but this time neither of us leans in or away.

'Can I ask you something?'

'Well, you just did.'

I give Diego a glowering stare.

'You know what I mean.'

'Shoot.'

I crane my neck again so that I don't have to look him in the eye, and wish we were laying floorboards or mixing paint.

'What happened that day on the beach?'

Diego sighs and looks up too.

'Ah, Wally. Nothing happened.'

'I know, that's what I mean.'

He is silent for a moment. 'Look, it's complicated, okay. You're an amazing girl, but you're just so…you seem so innocent. And I'm… well, I'm not. Then there's all this shit you're going through. I didn't want to take advantage of you.'

'Are you more attracted to my mother?'

Diego laughs.

'Jesus!'

'Or do you… not like the way I look?'

'Can't a guy just be decent?'

I bite the inside of my lip, hard. I know that I should be grateful that Diego didn't woo me into bed, but I'm not. Maybe I wanted my body to feel disposable. Maybe I wanted something to sever me – whatever the soul stuff is that transferred from my father to the bird – from my skin. While I have never experienced it, I'm sure that kind of transcendental physical union exists, and that it must have the capacity to create a fundamental rift. So far in my limited sexual experience, men have only served a utilitarian purpose: to garner something, like knowledge, or to take something away, like boredom or pain. I've never been undone.

Sarah was the first body other than mine that I really knew. Even then, she felt like a continuation of me. When my hands ran over her curves I wondered if they weren't the farther off regions of my own body; the soft pebbles of her nipples from an unexplored shore of my own femininity. In childhood, we held hands, fell asleep on the lawn with our heads pressed together, felt the curl of the other's leg in the night. We had a foundation of touch so that, when we were fifteen, watching a movie on a mattress in my living room, her head dipped a little closer to mine and our mouths closed together. It was the most natural folding, as simple as a butterfly's wings closing. Limbs entangled under the blue-green glow of the screen, heavy breathing hushed beneath dialogue, we relished in the giddy thrill of one eye fixed on the hallway and one ear pricked for the sound of Jill's bedroom door. I climbed towards a climax that never came, instead hovering in that heady moment before completion, uncertain of the limits our desires could reach. In all the movies we watched, there was always a man's eyes squeezed shut, mouth slightly agape, a high-pitched groan before slumping backwards. We didn't know any other endings yet.

Sarah and I never really spoke about that night until we were on the cusp of a replay, just before she asked me to be her girlfriend; but then, as a teenager, I was unsure of what boundaries we had technically crossed. I felt like I was missing out on something sacred that the other girls in our grade talked about with increasing frequency. We resolved to lose our virginity to two unsuspecting boys at an end-of-year party. With the taste of vodka Cruisers on our lips, we embraced in solidarity before slinking off into separate bedrooms on the wiry arms of our admirers. The boys were gone by the morning. Slightly hung over, we compared notes at the bus stop and decided that while the pain was bearable, we didn't see what all the fuss was about. The boys took it surprisingly well when we told them that we had no interest in boyfriends, or even in friendship. Confused, and a little bit upset that they wouldn't get another attempt perhaps – but mostly relieved. They knew they were out of their depths with girls who used too many big words and had a whole repertoire of private jokes.

Nothing much changed at university. There were a few short-lived and unsatisfying flings before Sarah and I started our relationship. Then after we broke up there was only the confident Spaniard on my Europe trip. 'David,' he said his name was, a poet. Maybe it was true, but there was nothing poetic about him. He had a face so basic that he could have gone by any name. David worked at the Guggenheim and struck up a conversation when he heard an accent beneath my bumbling Spanish. He asked me to meet him after work, and, although I didn't find him very attractive, there was a certain glamour of the establishment that rubbed off on him. It was like at university when I heard that a professor had studied at Harvard or Yale and listened closer in their lectures in case they dropped a secret garnered from within those Ivy League walls.

David and I walked in circles around the gallery, the stark titanium shapes reflected in broken mirrors across the Bilbao estuary. I went back to his tiny studio apartment and inside he pushed his mouth into mine like he was eating an over-ripe stone fruit, trying to suck up every drop of juice.

When I pulled back, he laughed: 'The English are always so frigid.' I didn't even bother to correct him. My mind wandered at first, but my body soon responded to David's strong will, his strong hands. He was rough and gentle at once. His fingers did one thing, while his lips contradicted. When he pushed into me, I closed my eyes and saw Gerard Richter's seascapes fading into splatters of Yves Klein Blue. Did birds cross the sky? Or was it me floating there? I can't remember, but, if there were any aesthetic truths to be gleaned from David, it might have been that the greatest pleasures occur on some interim plane between the body, the image, and the imagination.

Sitting next to Diego, I don't know how to explain any of this, so I don't say anything more.

When he speaks again, Diego's voice is soft. 'Are we okay?'

'Yeah.'

He leans into me, and I rest my head on his shoulder, but this time the touch is not electric. It is inert, and easy, and maybe somehow better.

I look across the night and wonder how far we can see – to whose skies – and how we could even discern between the different latitudes and longitudes of darkness. I close my eyes, and the darkness is there too.

'Did you see that?' Diego asks.

'What?'

I open my eyes, and the immensity is new again.

He draws a line with his finger. 'A shooting star. It shot all the way across.'

'No.' I look for a trace of the stellar spark, but it has faded completely. 'I didn't see anything.'

Walking barefoot along the shore at Sandy Beach, I remember something that I haven't remembered for a long time.

My toes squelch through the mud and, when I look down, my feet are still mine, but they are much smaller. The dark mud becomes soaked golden sand, and I remember running back through the shallows, then the waves, pushing a heavy surfboard in front of me.

When I was ten, Grandma Sue taught me to surf. I can still recall her face clearly, all of her features scrunched into a big smile. She could never hide a single emotion behind that expressive face. That's why she had so many wrinkles. She said anyone who felt as much as she did was bound to be as crumpled as an old shirt, but that the trade-off was just fine with her. She said she'd rather be authentic than beautiful, and she contested 'all that rubbish they sell you about beauty' anyway. She never specified who *they* were, but I assumed them to be people who wouldn't understand the simple joys of surfing.

Grandma Sue's sun spotted hands held the side of the pastel pink board to keep me in place as the big waves passed. I felt diminutive bobbing on that eight-foot plank of fibreglass, the water lifting me up and putting me down again. A giddy seesaw. When the waves broke a few metres in front of us, foam leapt off their backs. Sometimes there were small rainbows caught in the spray. I remember how different the sea looked from the other side. Before, I'd only swum close to the shore where the waves reached towards the sky with white fists before pounding the sand – children shrieking and diving in dolphin arcs. Floating out there, I watched the water roll slowly forwards and, for the first time, had an instinct that the whole world breaths like this, with its whole body.

I loved to watch Grandma Sue as she examined the waves. Her lips moving in silent tongues, she spoke the aqueous language, knowing when the abundant mounds would form into crumbly peaks, and when they would retreat back into the glassy flats. When the right wave approached, she took hold of the back of the board to propel me forward. 'Now!' she sang, and, with her push, I sprang to my feet without letting my knees touch down, just as she had instructed me on the sand. I felt the exhilarating rush for a moment before I lost my balance and toppled sideways into the saltwater. On a few attempts, I positioned my feet just right, turned my hips, and glided across the face of the wave – features cut with rippling force – suspended between water and sky. Grandma Sue cheered from behind the white wall of water chasing me, and I raced on and on until it caught me, falling gleeful into the rush of green, clasping with flailing hands, but only paddling into the realisation that some precious things can't be held.

After Grandma Sue died, I stopped surfing. The ocean seemed bigger without her – more ominous. I needed her hands and her voice to guide me. When the waves rose up, I couldn't see out to the calm place. Jill never had any interest in the beach, nor the time to take me. Eventually, I stopped thinking about surfing altogether. When we moved closer to the city, it became the distant pastime of tanned men in magazines and girls with messy blonde hair. Even when I went to the beach, I visited calm inlets like Gordon's Bay where I wasn't reminded of that thrusting thrill.

As I round the bend to where the curlews are feeding, nostalgia grips me – not just for the act of riding on waves, but for the fearless child I was then. I wonder how many of my fears are a symptom of losing Grandma Sue, and which parts of me left with her.

My father is among the birds again today, but I don't talk to him. Instead, I watch as he digs his beak into the feathers on the underside of his body, grooming himself. His head sweeps to the left as he sifts between the feathers on his back and tail. To reach the underside of his chin, he lifts one of his legs, and scratches vigorously like a dog with an itch. I count the curlews, and scribble notes in my table, careful not to make too much noise as I rearrange the papers. I watch on as my father walks down to the edge of the water and crouches in the shallows. He dunks his head beneath the surface a few times, flicking the water from his beak down his back. As his tail feathers bob up and down, I lose track of time. I am immersed in this ritual: part dance, part chore. I notice that my father has gained weight. I know that means he is readying to depart, and I want to ask him when he will go, but today the silence between us seems impassable.

Watching him among the other curlews, I wonder what version of me threatens to fly away with my father. I am almost certain that I have never met her. I wonder if it is always like this when someone leaves us? A sad economy of the self where you can never get back more than what is taken away. Or it's not that these versions are taken away so much as they follow the departed as surely as shadows. An old letter or a photo will lead us through a door, down a path, onto a boat, or a runway to embark on some journey where in a hidden alcove a switch occurs and another person is sent back in our place. At other times, we seal these other selves off in boxes with trinkets – cardboard coffins that we store away, or ship out, or dump, in the hope that our new selves might be cleansed of the affliction of memory – though I am sure it rarely, if ever, works out like that.

When my father is done bathing, he stands and opens his wings wide. The brown tips of his feathers look singed by the hard sun behind. He shakes the excess water from his body, and his feathers fluff up, clean and bright. My throat aches, but I don't feel like crying today. Instead, I decide that it must be time to go back to Oji's.

Jill will be awake, and she will probably be wondering where I am. She decided to stay on a little longer after Christmas, and I'm not sure when she will be leaving, or if she is waiting for me to give in and go with her. Yesterday, she helped Oji and me lay the new garden beds down the sides of the house. She poured the soil between the thin pine perimeters and even got dirt under her nails. The tension between us, persistent as lantana, was slowly weeded out and stuffed into black garbage bags with the other unwanted shrubbery.

Walking back through the dark mud, on the golden sand, I turn once more. The bay lays flat, but I can still see Grandma Sue waving from behind the waves, except now the waves are getting bigger and the whitewash obscures her face.

My feet are small again, and I press up on my tiptoes to keep sight of her.

My father turns his head in my direction.

I lift my hand to wave, but I don't know if they can see me.

9

The harsh smell of melting paint and scorched wood.
'It's another fire,' Oji calls from beyond the front door.
'Much closer than last time. There is lots of smoke from over
the back.'

Jill and I get up from the couch where we are sitting watching
talk shows on TV, eating tuna sandwiches. Jill backs towards
the window, unable to look away from the psychiatrist dishing
out advice to two forlorn parents while their gothic teenage son
scowls at the camera. I'm not sure exactly what the problem
is. Apparently, he has a pet snake and has been refusing to go
to church, but there is no mention of guns or sacrificing small
animals. Although I suppose the snake might eat live mice.

'I got lucky with you,' Jill says. 'There was a little bit of dark
period with all that black eye shadow and the lip piercing, but,
really, you were a good kid.'

I run my tongue over the inside of my lip and feel the small
indent that has never healed completely. 'The lip piercing! Why
did you ever say yes?'

'You were very insistent, and, to be honest, it suited you.
Somehow you still managed to look sophisticated with a hunk
of metal in your face.'

'At sixteen, I don't think I was going for sophisticated.'

'I figured it was better to let you make your own mistakes,
plus, you try having a teenage girl. All those hormones. If I'd
said no, I would never have heard the end of it. Tears, screaming,
the whole nine yards.'

'Understandable.'

We both look towards the southern end of the island where
a dramatic eclipse of plumes obscures the sky. Oji is right – it is

much more intense than when the fire burned on Stradbroke. This time, I can taste it.

'What should we do?' I ask.

Flecks of ash are carried on the wind and fall like dark snow.

'Let me see what the emergency services are saying,' Jill takes out her phone and presses the keys. 'Shit, no signal.'

Janine Wright comes out from the house across the street. She is stick-thin and wearing cut-off denim shorts with a faded blue tank top. A cigarette hangs from her lips as she shouts over the barking dog.

Jill gives me a nervous look and mouths the word 'I-c-e.'

I slap her on the arm.

A police car is parked out the front of a house three doors down.

'They're saying to head into town, to the community centre.' Janine signals at the officer in uniform going door to door. 'We'll be heading off soon.'

Ben Wright races outside carrying a stereo system and loads it into the boot of his Toyota Corolla.

'What do you need that for?' Janine shouts.

'Because it's fuckin' expensive, Mum!'

'Watch your language!'

Janine raises her hands in despair towards Oji. 'The way young men talk to their mothers these days!'

Oji gives her a sympathetic nod. 'Thanks, Janine. We'll see you there.'

A second middle-aged officer comes out of the house to the left of us and sees that we are already in motion. He takes off his hat, nods, and runs a hand through his thinning hair.

'Good afternoon, Tom,' Oji says.

He doesn't stop to chat. 'You heard, did you? Community centre, alright?'

Oji nods, and Tom bypasses our house, striding across the lawn to the neighours on the right. A hot gust blows in.

The three of us go inside as Ben and Janine continue to squabble about what they can fit into the car. The thrill of danger creates a frenetic activity. Jill hurries to pack her suitcase. I put a few things from the clean-clothes basket into a backpack. In the kitchen Oji loads an esky with food and water.

Jill holds up some old blankets from the hallway closet. 'Do you think we should bring these?'

'Couldn't hurt,' Oji says. 'Who knows if we'll have to sleep there tonight.'

'I've got a change of clothes for you,' I say.

Standing in the hallway, I look at all the work that Oji and I have completed since I arrived. Panic rushes over me.

Oji comes out of his bedroom with a small black toiletries bag in his hand, sensing my unease. 'Don't worry. They'll get it under control. It's just a precaution.'

I nod.

'Ready?' Jill shouts from the front door.

I move towards the door, but I'm not ready at all. More hot wind blows in from outside, and I want to be pushed back down the hall. I want to say that I'll just wait it out here, or at least suggest that we do that thing that people do on the news when fire strikes, dousing the house with the garden hose. But deep down I know that neither Jill nor Oji will let me have my way. All I can do is hope that the wind will blow in the other direction, or that the firemen will put the flames out quickly, or that the rain will come again.

'Come on!' Jill urges.

Oji approaches behind me and leads me forward with a palm pressed against the small of my back.

The Honda Civic joins a convoy of cars headings towards the centre of town. Reaching the road near the jetty, I see four rural fire trucks roll down the plank of the moored vehicle ferry, as purposeful as ants.

'Must be pretty big,' Jill remarks from the backseat.

I squeeze my eyes shut. Oji reaches across from the driver's seat and pats my hand. Sucking in the dry air, my throat burns like the first time I smoked a cigarette with Sarah at the lookout between Maroubra and Malabar Beach.

The small hall overflows with people, and more try to bustle in through the open double doors. Nev Smith stands on a chair at the front of the room. The back of his fluorescent vest says that he is the chief of the local volunteer fire fighting service. He tries to make an announcement over the distorted PA system.

'There are extra ferries scheduled for the rest of the day to evacuate as many people as possible. We recommend leaving the island until the fire is contained and extinguished. Anyone who chooses to stay can bunk down here.'

'We should go,' Jill says.

A crew of elderly women from the Country Women's Association set up some trestle tables in the corner of the hall, arranging urns of hot water next to towers of styrofoam cups. Plastic Tupperware containers of coffee, sugar and teabags are laid out. The lady I see swimming at the pool sometimes opens two packets of Arnott's assorted creams and all the children swoop at once. Max and Milly are amid the horde but haven't noticed me. I look around nervously for their dad. He is nowhere in sight.

'I'll get us something to drink to calm the nerves,' Oji says.

Jill nods. 'Please.'

Oji politely makes his way through the crowd of children and doesn't even scold the chubby boy that tramples on his foot. When we are left alone, Jill pulls me into a tight hug.

'Let's go,' she pleads. 'It's not safe here, and I put our flights in credit. We can get the first one out of Brisbane tomorrow morning.'

'No,' I struggle from her grip. 'I'm not going to leave while the house is at risk of burning to the ground. What about Oji?'

Jill sighs and drops her hands to her side. 'I know you're close with Oji, but I think you've gotten so caught up in this island that you've forgotten about the real world.'

'This is real, to me.'

'What about Sarah?'

'Sarah is fine!'

Jill shakes her head. 'No, she isn't.'

My mother never really acknowledged our relationship. She continued acting towards Sarah the same way she had all my life, like she was a close friend and nothing more. I can't believe she is bringing it up now that it is convenient for her case.

'She still loves you, Wallace. You could still work it out…'

'You don't know anything…'

'Yes, I do. We spoke before I came here. She's hurting…'

I am taken aback that my mother has been talking to Sarah. I want to know where they saw each other, under what circumstances, but I don't give her the satisfaction of asking.

'Look, I'm staying. You should go. If you care so much about Sarah, then you go look after her.'

'I know it's been hard for you since your father died but…'

'My father isn't dead!'

'Wallace…'

'Just stop, okay. If you want to go, then just go.'

'Well, if you really don't want me here anymore.'

I remain silent.

Oji returns clasping three cups in an unsteady pyramid. I take one from him with shaking hands. He holds the other out towards Jill.

'Everything okay?'

Jill snatches the tea. 'Just fine.'

She turns on her heels and stalks towards where Nev is drawing the new ferry timetable on a whiteboard surrounded by people craning their necks to see.

I sigh. 'Sorry. My mother can be… dramatic.'

Oji pats my arm.

'She's just worried about you.'

'Well, she doesn't need to be. I've got you.'

Oji smiles. 'Yes, you do. But she's still your mum. She's allowed to worry.'

'Do you think the house is going to be okay?'

'I do,' Oji's forehead creases in thought. 'But you know what? It's just a house. They're just trees. It's just an island. Let it all burn if it wants to.'

'But...' My jaw drops.

Oji shrugs.

I look at his face; it is vacant. I suppose I haven't thought much about if Oji feels as affectionately towards the house as I do. I had just taken it for granted that he does. There is a hint of aloofness in his voice that catches me off guard, but I don't know how to press him further in this busy room. He is watching intently as the old women rally a group of men to move stacks of chairs and lay them out around the perimeter. Then, with a snap, he turns his head, and he is back to his usual self.

'Sorry, I'm just a bit tired. I didn't mean to be so doom and gloom,' he chuckles. 'It'll all be okay. For now, I should go help.' He pats me on the back. 'You want to come with me?'

I nod, relieved by the familiar and comforting solace of a task.

By evening, word circulates that the fire has claimed some houses on Glendale Road, but that it hasn't spread past Ruth Street.

A weighty smoke reaches across the whole island and filters into the hall. It feels like it has seeped inside my head so even my thoughts are hazy. I sit in a corner wrapped in a sleeping bag trying to listen to music, but nothing soothes me. My phone lights up with a message from Diego. He is on the mainland and heard about the blaze once he finished work for the day. His boss is putting the six workers from Russell Island up for the night in a hotel.

'The other guys are digging into the mini-bar, but I just wanted to make sure everything is okay.'

I tell him that yes; we're all fine, which is technically true. I don't tell him how scared I am, or that renovating the house with Oji has given me the only real sense of purpose I've ever felt. He replies with an image of a thumbs up, and I wish there was a neat pictorial way to encapsulate the feeling of dread in my gut. I bet the workers are counting their good luck at the unlikely event of getting a free hotel room on New Years Eve. I picture them bomb diving into the swimming pool, playing drinking games or poker into the early hours of the morning. I wonder what Diego is like when he is with a group of other men, and how many other versions of him I've never seen. I think about all the things I've learned about my father since arriving – his poems, his fables, his chants – and how complex people really are when you start to peel the layers back.

Tired of this train of thought, and all my other thoughts, I go outside to see if I can find Oji.

The air outside is so smoky that I have to squint to make out the shapes around me. Once I adjust, I see that Jill and Oji are talking near the empty children's playground. When it got dark, Kate rounded up all the kids so she could read to them from one of the Harry Potter books in a room just off the main hall, sleeping bags arranged like dominoes. Near the base of the slippery slide, Jill is gesticulating with her arms. Oji's hands are dug deep in his pockets as he looks down at the colourless sand. I wonder what they are talking about and circle around to get within earshot without them seeing me.

'You need to stop filling her head with these ideas,' Jill hisses.

'I don't know what you mean.'

'This nonsense that her father is a bird?'

'That wasn't me. That night at the dinner table was the first I'd heard her speak about that too. I told her a story that Aki was reading when he was sick, where the main character becomes a bird, but I didn't know that the idea had taken root. Or maybe it started before that? I just didn't want to discourage her – that's why I stopped the conversation.'

'What do you mean you didn't want to discourage her? Of course you should discourage her! This is exactly what I'm talking about. You are encouraging her delusions.'

Oji rebuts quietly. 'Maybe they aren't delusions. Who are we to say what's real and what isn't to a girl who has just lost her father?'

He leans against a pole, and Jill takes another step forward, standing over him.

'Come on. You can't be serious. Every time I try to talk to her about it, she just shuts me out. All the articles I read say that I can't just confront her with the truth, because that can be even more damaging. But I'm no psychologist. She needs professional help. She's avoiding anything that will ground her back in reality. She hasn't even signed the house papers. But maybe you're happy about that?'

Oji doesn't react to my mother's insinuation. 'Just give her time.'

'Why? So, she can spiral even more. She needs to get off this island. She needs to come home. You need to be honest with her. Tell her the truth about what really happened.'

Oji looks up now, head tilted to one side. 'As you probably know, Aki had different ways of dealing with things, too. He was her father after all. She might not see things exactly how you do.'

It is the most matter of fact I've heard him be with anyone, but his voice remains calm.

'I wish everyone would stop acting like fatherhood is some genetic right. He was never her father,' Jill replies.

Jill crosses her arms across her chest and Oji looks beyond her, as if he is carefully choosing his words. I worry for a moment that he will see me, but his eyes scan right past the trees.

'But... I wonder... How much of that is because you wouldn't let him be?'

Jill's eyes open wide. 'What are you talking about?'

'Well, wasn't Aki honest with you about his sexuality?'

'What does that have to do with anything?'

'Wasn't he following your wishes by leaving?'

'That's what he said, is it? What kind of life would that have been for us? Living a lie with a man who doesn't want you? To have him there but always wishing he was somewhere else? We were together for two years before Wallace was born. Did you know that? I thought we were building a life together, here. He met my mother. My mother actually liked him! My mother had never liked anyone I bought home. Do you know how humiliating that was for me? Finding out I'd been living a lie for two years. But then, his whole life was a lie.'

Oji is silent for a moment. 'Of course, I wasn't there. I'm not presuming to know. But what about Wallace... what about...' Oji closes his eyes and mumbles something in Japanese under his breath, trying to translate what he wants to say to inflict the least offense.

'*Urusai! Kankai nai desho!*'

Oji opens his eyes wide and looks struck by the strangely familiar words that have escaped my mother's lips. I can't believe what I'm hearing either.

'You speak Japanese?' he asks.

A strange sound gurgles up from inside me. Almost animal. Jill spins around, probably expecting to see a bird or a small mammal. I step from the shadows.

'Mum!' I exclaim.

'Wallace!'

Suddenly, my face is hot with tears. All the times that I told Jill I wanted to learn Japanese, she brushed me off and suggested I try something easier, more cultured, like Spanish or French.

What good would Japanese do an artist? All these years, she has been hiding my language in her own mouth. Then there is what Oji said about her sending my father away, the fact that they were together for two years, that he told her that he was gay. There is so much new information that my temples throb trying to process it all.

A scene with Grandma Sue flashes in my mind. There was a book with a cartoon picture of a Japanese girl on the cover. She wore a kimono, and her eyes were drawn with triangles tipped on their sides. It was a children's book for learning hiragana. Grandma Sue and I sat on the balcony as she helped me make sense of the lines that were nothing like our letters.

'*Shi*. She has beautiful long hair.'

Grandma Sue pointed to the image of the curled line, like a fishing hook, included in an image of a girl's silhouette. The line was accentuated with a thick black stroke to make up the girl's long locks – the rest of the image of her face was shaded in light grey. The idea was that, every time I saw the symbol for *Shi*, I would remember the girl with the beautiful long hair and recall its name.

'*Shi*,' I repeated. 'She has beautiful long hair.'

'Good, well done.'

Next, Grandma Sue pointed at two black dashes, drawn into a circle with a dollar sign at the centre.

'*Ko*, a gold coin.'

I squeezed my eyes shut and memorised the image.

'*Ko*,' I repeated. 'A gold coin.'

Jill appeared in the doorway, and I could feel her watching us.

'What are you up to?'

'Learning Japanese!'

'Well, enough of that for now, it's time for dinner. Go wash your hands.'

I obediently closed the book and went inside. From the bathroom, I could hear my mother and grandmother arguing in hushed tones. Later, when I asked Grandma Sue if we could finish our lesson, she told me some other day, and I never saw the book again.

'Wallace, I can explain... I just know a few words. From when...'

'Don't bother,' I sob. 'Please just leave.'

Oji stands frozen in place.

'Wallace,' Jill steps towards me with an arm outstretched but I slap it away.

'Go!' I scream. 'Just go!'

I bury my face in my hands, and, when I remove them, I am pressed against the softness of Oji's shirt. I can hear my mother speaking, but I can't make out what she is saying over my own sobs. When I stop and lift my face to suck in some air, she is gone. The park is empty except for Oji and me. I lean into him again and he holds onto me with a firm circle of arms, like he is holding a bundle of sticks together.

From the corner of my eye, I see the outdoor sensor lights of the community centre turn on, and then, after a minute, they flick off again. I can smell sausages cooking somewhere. Someone inside is strumming a guitar.

'10, 9, 8, 7, 6, 5, 4, 3, 2, 1!'

Just like that, another year begins.

The trees lining the beach are charred black.

Peter walks in front carting the tracking devices and nets. I follow behind with the two bamboo poles under my arm.

'Are you sure you're feeling up to this?'

'Yes,' I assure him. 'I'm fine.'

Peter talks over his shoulder, 'I'll be surprised if many of the birds have come back here after a scare like that. You got lucky, 'ey?'

'Yeah, really lucky.'

Oji and I arrived home later on New Year's night to find the house as we'd left it. Just a thin layer of grey ash settled on the deck. Silently, he filled a bucket with water, and, before we even took off our shoes, we cleaned the soot away – him with the mop, and me wiping down the awnings and the outdoor furniture with an old rag. There were no lights on in the whole street, and only the sound of water sloshing from the bucket. I don't think anyone else had come home yet. There was quite a party kicking on at the community centre, but Oji and I slipped out.

Inside, we belatedly toasted with the leftover wine from Christmas poured into champagne glasses and fell asleep in the living room watching replays of the fireworks display from Sydney on TV. I was exhausted but relieved to be back. Drifting off to sleep, I smiled at the roman blinds that we wrestled with for hours to get in the right position, an orange cushion hugged close to my chest. I knew that in the morning the cushion would need to be washed along with everything else, but right then, everything was perfect.

I woke up when Oji snored a little, and, in the early dawn glow, shook his shoulder and guided him towards his bedroom. Inside my own room, I curled up and fell into a deep sleep; I didn't wake until almost noon.

That was a few days ago and the house has been mostly returned to its pristine state. This morning when I woke up though, I found some stray ash behind the sugar jar and wiped it away with a cloth. Peter came around as I finished washing my breakfast dishes and we set out towards Sandy Beach. As we rounded the bend and headed towards the bay I watched for the precise moment when the foliage changed. At the base of the hill the firemen must have halted the blaze because on one side of the street blackened remains jutted from ash-covered soil, and on the other, the tree bark was singed, but the leaves still clung to the branches. The trunks seemed to slant away from the road a little, as though they tried to flee from the flames and were confronted by their own immobility.

Missed call Sarah

Missed call Jill

Missed call Unknown

I take out my phone to check the time and see that the notifications are piling up again. I sent Sarah a message yesterday to wish her a happy new year, and she's been calling ever since. I didn't send Jill anything, but, still, she calls, too. I suppose she must be back in Sydney. Oji said that he spoke to her before we left the community centre on New Year's night, and she planned to get the first ferry in the morning, to give me some space. I didn't say goodbye. As for Robert Waters, the lawyer, I know that I can't avoid him for much longer.

The low tide has left uneven pools spread across the beach. I put my phone back in my pocket, nestling the bamboo poles awkwardly in my armpit, as Peter and I keep walking. Our boots slosh down into the glassy craters.

'The uni came through with the extra funding for another couple of trackers. So, we've got to get them on before the birds head off.'

I try to mask the anxiety in my voice. 'When will they go?'

'Some will head off soon; the rest will be gone by February or March. Depending on the weather.'

When we reach the section of beach where we set the mist nets last time, Peter drops his pack with a groan and stretches his back.

'Right, you remember what to do?'

I nod and take one of the bamboo poles to the other end of the clearing and wriggle it into place, then I walk back to where Peter is standing with the second pole erect. I help him attach the nets.

135

'Now, the good old waiting game.'

Peter squats in the rough marram grass and opens his bag. I prop myself on a rock.

'Do you want to see some of the data we've got so far?'

I nod enthusiastically. 'Please.'

Peter pulls out a folder and flicks through the plastic sheets until he reaches some satellite images.

'Look,' he says pointing at the page. 'This is a map of the area, and these points,' he prods the dots, 'are where this particular bird has been since we put the tracker on.'

I look closely at the aerial map of Redland Bay and its surrounds. The yellow dots and connecting lines form a messy constellation. The first bird has visited twenty or more sites, some further inland than I would have expected, but the majority land along the edges of the bay and its islands.

'This is fascinating.'

Peter smiles. 'I know, right? Look at this one.'

He flicks the page and shows the same map but with a different assemblage of dots and lines. This curlew has visited just as many sites, but they are much more condensed. The constellation forms a diamond shape. Peter turns the page again.

'Then, this one is really interesting.'

The third curlew's sites when joined together look like an isosceles triangle. It has only visited three locations: the island and two points at either end of the bay.

'Much more site fidelity. It's intriguing how different they all are. I should probably know why. I'm sure your father would have explained it to me. But I'll have to start hitting the books more.'

It is amazing to see weeks of an animal's life compressed into two dimensions – its every movement condensed into raw data then spat out as an image.

Peter closes the folder. 'How are you doing, anyway?'

I nod. 'Okay.'

The coffee from his thermos is steaming hot. He pours some into a metal cup and hands it to me. We both sip slowly and stare at the green foliage of Stradbroke protected from the fire by the moat of the bay. It is no longer a mirror image.

'I guess I'm just a bit sad. For the birds. They already have so much to deal with.'

Peter nods. 'I know what you mean.'

He takes another sip of his coffee.

'That reminds me, there's this story Mat told me.'

I wait patiently for Peter to speak again. Like Oji, he sets his own pace, and, even though I really want to hear the story, I know there's no use in trying to hasten him.

'It is about a guy called Henare Hāmana. You might have heard of the Huia bird from New Zealand? Or maybe not. They're extinct now, but you can still find the sound of their call on the Internet, or a good imitation of it, at least. Hāmana, this Maori guy, was recorded singing the bird's song for the radio back in '54.'

I brush away a small swarm of sand flies resting on my arm. 'Why?'

Peter laughs. 'Good question. The New Zealand government was concerned that the birds might be going extinct and sent out expedition parties to gather live specimens, accompanied by local Maori guides. One of them was Hāmana. They didn't find anything. So, when people realised that saving the species was pretty much out of the question, they wanted to hold onto something, and I guess the call was the best they could think of.

A radio station invited Hāmana in to whistle the ditties he remembered from his childhood. When you listen, the guy on the radio sets the scene... Peter puts on his best mock radio voice, '*Let us imagine two birds feeding in a tree, after a while the female climbs to the top of the tree and flies into the distance. The male bird calls with the following notes...* Hāmana whistled into the recorder. When I first heard it, it stopped me in my tracks. It was one of the most startling things. Otherworldly, really. Listening to the sound of this dead bird through the vocal cords of this dead man, travelling to me across who knows what signals and waves. Then, I was the saddest I had been since, since I don't know when. Since my wife passed away, I suppose. Because I knew that no one – not me or anyone else –would ever hear that sound in real life again. It was like looking at a replica of a beautiful painting, while knowing the original had gone up in flames.'

I think about the magnificent floral De Heem painting at the Art Gallery of NSW that I saw when I first arrived back in Sydney. Surveying the skeletal trees along the beach, I think about how much time De Heem must have spent staring at vases of flowers, contemplating mortality. I wonder if he watched the flowers wilt, and whether he had to spray them with a fine mist to prolong their life. Or, if they sometimes succumbed to their droopy fates before he finished his projects. I wonder what he did with all the dead flowers, and, if in the nick of time, he ever gifted them to a woman so they would wither on her nightstand instead of in his studio. Or, if he ever woke in her bed after a night of passionate lovemaking to see the turning bouquets in the early morning glow, and whether he felt guilty for plucking them from the living world?

Thinking about the fate of the flowers in the painting, I am sad, but I am sad twice over. I hope that De Heem realised that, for the flowers, being immortal and being dead were one and the same. If he did realise, I wonder if he ever spared a thought for the fact that his canvases too were mortal, that they could one day be consumed by fire, or decompose, on a much greater time scale of course, but that they would eventually meet the same fate. I think he must have thought about it a lot, and that's why he painted the window. He knew that no matter how many beautiful flowers he painted, he couldn't alleviate his own fear of death and sometimes it all felt so bleak that even when staring inwards, he just needed to look outside.

Peter's voice brings me back to the beach.

'Yeah, so, when I saw your Dad that last time we did a count, we talked about the idea of preservation. He was fascinated by the story. He told me he had started practicing his own curlew calls. I asked him to demonstrate for me, and he was getting pretty good, actually.'

'Really?'

I picture my father sitting in the same spot as me, calling like a bird.

'Yeah,' Peter nods. 'And now since he's been gone, I can't help trying to pick his voice out from the bunch. When I hear that cry, I just hope with all my might that my grandkids won't be listening to some old codger like me singing when all the birds are gone.'

He screws the lid back onto his coffee thermos. 'Anyway, I'm babbling… have you got your notebook?'

I nod and rummage in my bag for it. The photo of my father and me falls out onto the ground. I pick it up and show it to Peter.

'You would have known him then, right?'

Peter takes the photo and his face lights up.

I study my father's features closely and wonder if he was harbouring a bird inside him for all those years like a parasite that eventually takes control of its host, or if he made the choice to transform all on his own?

I look at the image upside down in Peter's hands, and then at the two curlews that have landed on the flats. Neither of them is my father. My throat is tight. I think about the coordinates on the map, and how soon more dots will be added like a satellite zooming out as the birds get further and further away.

'Peter,' I say.

'What is it, love?'

I run my finger over the image of my father's face.

'Wallace, are you okay?'

Peter reaches out and stills my hand. I look up at him, my eyes brimming with tears.

'Peter,' I sob. 'I don't want them to go.'

'It's okay,' Peter says softly.

I grip the photo and sob louder, my shoulders trembling.

Two birds fly into the mist net and release sharp squawks. I turn my head to see their wings contorting against the fine mesh. Their claws stick out through the holes as they struggle. Peter ignores the commotion and takes the image from my hands. He places it back inside my notebook, puts the book in my bag, and rests a hand on my shoulder.

'That's it,' he says. 'Let it out, love. Let it all out.'

10

Some days I ride the ferry in circles to kill time.
The service is free when travelling between the islands, and, if I don't depart at Redland Bay, Joe never asks me to show a ticket as he checks all the boarding passengers. Some days, I only do one loop; on others, I do two, or three – it depends on what Oji and I are working on at the house. There is much less to do now that the renovations are nearly finished.

When Janine Wright came to borrow a cup of sugar the other day, she complimented the colour scheme and said it was almost catalogue worthy.

'A K-Mart catalogue,' I joked.

Even though the décor is economical, everything looks matching and sleek.

The brown blinds offset the camel throw rug. There is a wooden bowl on the coffee table that holds some glass oranges with no other purpose than to balance the feature wall.

If Oji and I decide to sell the house, I am sure we will make a nice profit, but we don't want to sell it – I don't think. It hasn't come up in conversation, but I think we are in agreement. What would I say if Oji did want to sell and go back to Japan? I don't know, and hope I won't find out. I haven't been to count the birds at all this week, so I have spent most afternoons on the ferry. Peter told me to take some time off, to clear my head.

Yesterday, while gliding between Macleay and Karagarra Islands, I finally spoke to Robert Waters from the law firm in Brisbane.

'Wallace McKenzie!' he exclaimed when he heard my voice. 'I was beginning to wonder if I was ever going to get a hold of you.'

'Yeah, sorry, I've been… busy.'

The excuse sounded weak, but Robert charged on as if he'd heard it all before. His voice boomed like a used car salesman's, and, from the way he shrugged off the fact that I had been blatantly avoiding him for months, I concluded that I'm probably not his most difficult client.

'Look, it's not a problem. You already know that you've been left your father's share in the house, right? There's no mortgage so you don't have to worry about banks. I just need to know which address I can send the paperwork to? Where are you located at the moment?'

'I'm at the house, actually. Well, not right now. But that's where I'm staying.'

'Oh,' Robert laughed. 'Well, had I have known that, this could have been done and dusted by now.'

'Yeah. I've been a little distracted.'

'Yes, of course,' his voice became more formal then, as though he had just recalled the nature of our business. 'I'm sorry. I'll express post the forms to you today, and if you can send them right back with a signature, I'll get them processed. No need to draw things out any longer.'

His words stayed in my head after I hung up the phone. There really wasn't a need to draw things out any longer. It was all very simple, really. My father and all the birds would soon be gone. He'd left me half a house, but it didn't change anything. I would soon need to go back to my old life, and all of this would fade from my mind. I'd be the same fatherless girl that I had always been.

Russell Island grows smaller as the ferry moves out into the bay. The southern end is barren, desiccated branches jutting out over the tideline. The sun blazes down and urchins of white light move below the surface of the water. I survey the banks of Lamb Island as the ferry moors. On the nearby flats, a curlew cries.

From the river, I hear voices, like souls abandoned; curlews are calling. Curlews are calling.

Yesterday, I came upon an English opera on YouTube called *The Curlew River*. The idea of abandoned souls trapped in the cry of a bird reminded me of Peter's story about the Huia bird, so I scribbled the line in my notebook. I still spend a lot of time scouring the Internet for information about curlews. I am not sure what I am hoping to learn, but I have noticed that nearly everything I read leads me back to a paper by, or an interview with, my father. Not the opera, though. It was a welcome break from laments about ecological devastation. I watched the amateur rendition from start to finish, the crackly video recorded on a handheld camera. My favourite character was the madwoman who was in fact played by a fat and balding man. Later I read that the opera was based on a fifteenth century Japanese Noh play, so I supposed the casting had something to do with tradition. In the original, the birds weren't curlews at all, but small Miyako songbirds. Though, in both versions, the sentiment remained the same – the birds acted as messengers between the worlds of the living and the dead.

Watching Joe resting on the big ship wheel, I recall the ferryman in his boat traversing the river that separates the marshy banks of the east from the kingdom in the west. *Dividing person from person.* Then there was the soul of the dead boy trapped inside the yew tree, his cries from the otherworld indistinguishable from those of the curlew. His poor mad mother crossing the river only to find out that her son had already been dead for a year, and, although she wanted to speak with him so badly, she was too wretched with grief to commune with the birds or his spirit. She howled and howled while the shipmen and townspeople ridiculed her.

Wild birds, I cannot understand your cry.

The ferry engine rumbles into action again as we push away from the jetty. Over the rough hum of the propeller cutting through the water, I can't hear the curlews anymore, and I'm glad. Last week, I dreaded to think of them leaving; of each day going to the beach to find their numbers less and less, until one day there was just none there at all. But now I think I just want this whole strange chapter to be closed. I look up at Joe. If he thinks I am crazy, riding in circles around the bay, he doesn't say so. He is nothing like the ferryman in the play.

'Beautiful day to be out on the water, ey?'

He removes his large hands from the wheel and opens them wide, as though picking up the whole vista and presenting it to me.

I nod and feign a smile.

Grey tufts of hair from his chest stick out of his shirt collar – his pale calves jut from his khaki shorts as he taps a brown leather moccasin in time with the seventies rock playing quietly in the cabin.

Turning back to the route ahead, he gives me a wink.

An unhurried strum fills the backyard.

Diego sits on a chair sliding his fingers across the frets of his guitar. From the picnic blanket, I continue thumbing through a magazine, pretending not to listen intently. He isn't playing a song, or at least not one with a discernible melody; he seems to choose a chord at random, and then follows it up with another complementary sound, then another.

I take the last bite of the arepa with egg in the middle that Diego made for lunch.

He talks while he plays. 'Do you like it? I used to eat an arepa every morning when I was a child, except they were much better than these. The family on the corner had a cart and cooked them fresh over coals. My mother bought them before she went to work at the market.'

'Delicious,' I say, inspecting the white crispy tortilla-like dough.

Diego shrugs. 'They're lacking that smoky flavour, and

the flour isn't quite right, but it's the best I can do with the ingredients here.'

I scoop up the last pieces of egg that have fallen on to my plate and lick my fingers. 'Que rico!'

Diego laughs. 'Que rrrrico.'

I try again, rolling my tongue against the roof of my mouth, but the *r* gets caught in my throat.

Diego shakes his head and returns to strumming, but this time progresses into a refrain that sounds like it might be a Latin folk song. Leaning back on my arms, I sway my feet and look up at the sky. The weather is fine; the chalky clouds seem miles away.

'You're good,' I say. 'Play another.'

Diego grins. 'In a minute. Do you want a beer?'

I shake my head.

Diego goes into the house, and I can hear him chatting with Oji. I lie on my back and rest my arms behind my head, elbows propped out to the side. I close my eyes and waves of brick-red light roll by. My skin tingles with warmth. The smell of pollen and cut grass. I survey my body for feelings and thoughts, but there is nothing pressing that I need to attend to. I am still confused about what I'm supposed to do next, but I don't feel the need to resolve my anguish right now.

Since Jill left, Oji and I have settled back into our routine. He hasn't pushed me to talk about what I heard during the fire, and I haven't bought it up. Diego doesn't know that Jill and I had a fight; he thinks she just went home, so he doesn't pry either. We have been spending more time together, afternoons like these. I enjoy Diego's company. When he is around, I don't think too much about my father, or my mother, or the curlews. He makes me laugh.

Diego's footsteps pat against the lawn, the hiss of the can, a deep gulp, then the soft tap of wood as his guitar is propped on his knee again. Wordlessly, tenderly, the notes resume. When the song finishes, I sit up suddenly. I am not sure why the idea hasn't occurred to me until now.

'You should play at Laura's exhibition!' I say. 'We still don't have anyone, and you're really talented!'

Diego shakes his head. 'Thanks, but no thanks.'

'Don't make us use Kate's playlists! Please?'

He grins. 'You know I used to be in a band?'

'Really?'

He nods. 'When I was in my teens. Back home.'

'What were you called?'

'Los Rancheros. It's so embarrassing. It was a terrible name. And we played terrible music. Rock, punk.'

'What does it mean?'

'Funnily enough, it's something like 'The Farmers.' My mum used to love to play ranchero tracks in the house, and we were rebelling against the old school or something like that. Anyway, we eventually stopped because we found out some other band in Argentina had the same name, and they were much better than us.'

I laugh. 'Did you have a Mohawk?'

He hides his face in his palms. 'No, sideburns.'

'No way!'

Diego looks out into the bush as he remembers his youthful transgressions, and I try to imagine him young and wild with a rockabilly haircut, thrashing at his guitar, screaming into a microphone as sweat soaked through his torn t-shirt.

'So, is that a yes?'

Diego gives me a confused look.

'To playing at the exhibition?'

He doesn't answer, just starts strumming again, maniacally this time.

'Well, you can't play that,' I tease.

He races on, faster and faster.

Oji shouts from the back step. 'Everything alright out there?'

Diego plays on, while I put my hands over my ears.

'Make him stop!'

Oji chuckles. 'Don't make me come down there, kids!'

Diego's thrashing unsettles the cockatoos sitting in the trees just beyond the fence. They take off over our heads in a saintly flash of white and yellow.

The courtyard at the back of Kate's café is lit with threads of fairy lights. The space is open air, but there is a roof constructed from clear corrugated plastic with a mesh underlay, almost completely covered by a dense vine.

People steadily stream in, and I notice Laura sitting in a chair in the back corner chewing her fingernails. I make my way to the table covered in a white cloth where the wine and cheese are and pour two glasses of white. Roberta is talking with her husband by the stage and gives me a wave. Julie (or is it Christina?) laughs loudly at something Megan Riley has said. I edge my way around them. Laura doesn't notice me approaching.

'How are you doing?'

She jumps and grimaces. 'Nervous, does it show?'

'A little,' I hand her a glass of wine. 'Drink this.'

She takes a sip and stands to survey the faces coming in through the narrow entryway. There are so many people I have never seen before, or perhaps, I just don't recognise them in their evening attire.

'It's a good turn out,' I raise my glass and Laura clinks hers gingerly.

'People love an excuse to get dolled up.'

'Come on!' I scold. 'You're good, and you know it.'

Laura is wearing a slinky black dress that accentuates her small frame. Her hair is ironed completely straight, and her lips are shaded in an edgy bright orange.

'Plus, you're a babe. Every prince charming on the island is probably coming to try and win your hand.'

147

She playfully slaps my arm. 'Stop it! You know I have a strict rule about dating island men. I like to keep my suitors separated by a deep moat.'

We laugh.

Kate is making her way through the crowd, greeting everyone, her flowing boho skirt skimming the ground. When she spots us, she comes over.

'Already sold one!'

Laura's jaw drops. 'What?'

I nudge her in the ribs. 'I told you.'

Kate nods. 'The *Petrichor*. We'll have to give Oji a free tea for the name, hey?'

Laura smiles and starts to relax.

Alice Coltrane chimes spangle through the speakers and I look at my watch nervously. I hope Diego hasn't backed out. On cue, he enters the courtyard carrying his guitar, his curly hair pulled back into a short ponytail.

I excuse myself from Kate and Laura and go to greet him.

'Right on time,' I smile.

Diego tries to keep his eyes on mine, but I catch him stealing a glance at my outfit: a duck-egg blue midi dress cinched at the waist, the skirt overlaid in thin lace. I am lucky I packed one nice dress. I suppose I imagined the island would be a little livelier. It is nice to have an excuse to wear it.

Diego gives a whistle, picks up my hand and twirls me. 'Someone scrubs up alright.'

I laugh. 'Professionalism! We're working, remember?'

Diego tenses his face. 'Right. You're right, Miss Mackenzie. Where do you want me?'

I lead him over to the small stage made of old pallets covered in a heavy black sheet. A small wooden stool sits in the centre in front of a microphone stand.

'Don't move too much while you're up there.'

'Are you trying to kill me?'

'I guarantee it's perfectly safe… provided you stay still.'

Diego laughs. 'I'll try that one with my boss next week when I'm putting up the scaffolding.'

He unlatches his case, takes out the beech-coloured guitar with gold frets, and leans against a table to tune up. I see Oji talking to Terry Bennet a few feet away.

'I'm in trouble because I forgot our anniversary last week, but I'm going to make it up to her with a trip over to the casino… they say money can't buy love, but I don't know if they've met my wife.'

Oji chuckles, and I grab his elbow. Oji gives Terry a friendly slap on the back, turning away.

'Wallace this is wonderful,' he embraces me warmly. 'A real shin-dig, or so Terry says, but I don't quite understand that expression. A dig in the shins doesn't sound like fun.'

I laugh. 'Well, I didn't do much.'

'Don't listen to her,' Kate interrupts from over my shoulder. 'She did nearly everything.'

Oji doesn't respond because the nearest painting – a floral mandala filled with vibrant oranges and yellows – has caught his attention.

'Wouldn't this look great in the living room, Wallace?'

I turn to inspect the picture and nod. The painting is a big step up from the mass-produced prints sold in department stores, or motivational quotes on blocks of wood – both of which Oji has suggested as alternatives. I leave the circle as Diego strums quietly to himself, and Oji and Kate start discussing the price.

'Don't forget to haggle for a discount. You named the top-seller after all,' I joke, excusing myself.

I am feeling overwhelmed by all the company and conversation, so I head towards the exit to get some fresh air.

Outside, the breeze lifts the edges of my dress. Crossing the car park, the chatter from inside becomes distant and amorphous. I keep walking across the grass that leads down to the jetty. There is no one else around, just the sound of a few latecomers' car doors closing.

Near the entry to the jetty, I take a seat on a wooden bench. The dark purple water gleams like a slick of oil. Down on the flats, a few steps below, I hear a rustle. A curlew emerges from the shadows. I lean forward to see it more clearly in the fluorescent light filtering from above the ferry timetable.

'It's you,' I say with a sharp breath.

The bird turns its head and looks at me, then pecks the ground once.

'I thought maybe you'd already gone.'

I look up at the clouds passing in front of the moon. From the corner of my eye, I see the bird peck the ground twice. It's just a coincidence, I try to tell myself, if you want to believe anything badly enough, you'll find patterns to support your *delusions,* as Jill called them. The bird keeps standing there, staring at me. It doesn't flinch or move as the wind picks up, rustling the surrounding trees.

'What are you doing here? What do you want from me?'

I feel agitated. Why did it have to come tonight? Just when everything was starting to feel normal again? With slow purposeful steps, the curlew walks in my direction. It strides up the concrete steps, onto the walkway, right over to the bench where I am sitting. It is so close I can see the individual colours of its feathers, just like when I watched it through the binoculars. Its wings are mottled like slabs of bark. I am frozen in place. Not because I am afraid – I have never heard of anyone being attacked by a curlew – but because I don't know what to do. The curlew lifts its beak so that it can look at me again, and I see that it's still him. There's no way I can deny it, not to myself.

The bird lowers its head towards the ground and pecks twice, emitting a flat sound. I shake my head, tears filling my eyes.

'Could you just stop it? I'm wearing makeup and it's going to get ruined if I start crying.'

The bird stays where it is, unmoving. It is so close that I could kick it with my polished boot if I wanted to.

'The most annoying thing is, that I don't know what to believe. I think I wanted so badly to know my father that I could have conjured him into just about anything. Someone could have told me his soul was inside a dog, or a horse, or even a tree. He could have been inside a refrigerator, and I would have listened to the hums it made in the night. But, of course, a bird makes the most sense. I understand all of that. But, when I look at you, I know that he's in there… that you're in there… Dad… somehow, I can't explain it… I just…'

As I look down, the bird inches forward again. Closer and closer, until its head is pressing against my thigh and its beak is laid across my legs. All my muscles tense. It tilts its head upwards slightly to meet my gaze. I can't believe what is happening. I look around to see if there is anyone nearby, but the park and the jetty are empty.

After a moment, the curlew lowers its gaze again and presses into me more firmly. The underside of its chin is soft; its beak feels like a stick laid over my lap. My fists are clenched tightly at my side, but I un-ball them, and stroke the back of the bird's neck with an open palm. It doesn't move away, but I can feel its body tremble under my touch. The feathers on top of its head are downy and warm. I don't know how long we stay like that. Time is measured only by the rise and fall of my wrist.

'What am I doing? What the hell am I doing?'

My question curls up into the night, and the spell is broken when I hear a loud cheer, and a guitar starts to strum back up at the café.

'I should get back,' I whisper.

The bird steps away from me as I stand to my feet.

'But will I see you before you go?'

Once more, a single peck.

When I re-enter the courtyard, Diego is tapping against the wood of his guitar to bring in his next song. He flicks his nails across his strings sharply, and then fingers an intricate melody. The soul of flamenco but gliding like jazz.

'He's good,' Laura says into my ear.

I nod as Diego sees me and gives us a wink.

'And single,' I tease.

Laura laughs. 'Island man!'

I shrug my shoulders mischievously.

'Sorry we started without you,' she adds. 'We couldn't find you.'

'That's okay, I had to take a phone call,' I lie.

As the song increases in tempo, Kate joins us, and hands me a fresh glass of wine. I don't mention the bird, or the unexpected weight of its head, but, when I lift my glass to my mouth, I can still smell the musty scent of its feathers. I take a sip and move my hips slowly in time with the music. The space in front of the tiny stage becomes a dance floor as bodies brush against each other. Kate lifts her arms with serpentine flow.

'Thanks so much for your help, Wallace.'

'It's been fun,' I say as Laura sidles between us and grabs my hand.

'You'll be going soon then, I suppose?'

'I suppose.'

My words are wrapped in the final notes, then drowned out by applause.

11

My father is a candle. My father is a flame. My father is a knot in the oak bookcase. My father is a bottle of Suntory whiskey. My father is a pawn. My father is a knight. My father is a bird drawn in brown pencil. My father is a Kookaburra laughing like my grandmother.

The books are lined up so perfectly that they might be painted onto a flat board, concealing a secret alcove behind. On a fold-out bar tucked between the shelf and the coffee table, there is a half empty bottle of whiskey, a decanter, and two crystal glasses. From what I can gather, the room is still just as my father left it. I try to conjure him into the space, reclining in the chair, a book open on his lap, but I can't.

Oji is crouched on the floor with his back to me taking the leather-bound books off the lower shelf and placing them into a cardboard box. I see the Yeats compendium disappear beneath a guide to the plants of Borneo and feel a pang. I haven't made it through the whole collection, and I wonder what other secrets about my father could be hiding inside all these pages, soon to be sealed away. The heavy curtains are drawn to block the harsh afternoon sun, but it is still hot inside the office. I finish taping the bottom of another box and join Oji.

When I asked him the other day what he wanted to do with the space, he said he'd like to turn it into a gymnasium. I wasn't sure if he was joking or not, but he flexed his fleshy arm.

'I'll waste away to nothing otherwise.'

I nodded and helped him look at secondhand gym equipment online.

'Peter could bring some things in his ute,' I suggested.

Oji smiled gratefully. I liked the idea of him exercising. He is going to need to do something to keep himself active once the renovations are done. My father's office is the last room that we need to work on. I am nervous about finishing but am also proud of everything we have accomplished. February is only a few days away; the last three and a half months of my life will soon be archived in every layer of paint, nail, glossy surface.

This morning at the breakfast table, Oji and I formulated our plan for the next few days: to empty out and pack all my father's belongings, paint the walls with a fresh coat of white paint, and lay the same floating floors as the living areas. Once Oji's box is full of books, he stands to tape it up shut and pushes it out into the hallway. When he comes back, he goes over to the large mahogany desk and starts throwing the stationary into a garbage bag without even testing if the pens work. He opens the drawers, and I can hear the rattle of small objects – keys, coins, paper clips – as he sorts through them.

I run my finger along the spines of the remaining books. I scroll over four or five books quickly, as if I might be able to glean the knowledge of my father's collection at rapid speed. Then, I stop suddenly at an old and tattered spine, the familiar shape of the embossed title catching my eye. *The Malay Archipelago* by Alfred Russel Wallace. The hard brown cover is cracked; the stitching adjoining the columns of pages is exposed in places. I take the book out carefully and sit in the armchair next to the coffee table, opening to an earmarked page.

Alfred Russel Wallace is in Sarawak trying to hunt a large male orangutan with a group of Dyak men. I read the passage, looking over at Oji to see if he will scold me for slacking off, but he is deeply immersed in his task. I learn that so far on the expedition Alfred has already shot several specimens but is bitterly disappointed because they all turned out to be female: '*Not nearly so remarkable as the full-grown males.*' On this particular day, he stands before a tall tree and takes aim at an orangutan moving among the branches. He shoots once and makes impact, but the animal continues to climb. He shoots again and connects, but the orange mound rolls over, gets up, and begins to climb again. With the third shot, the lumbering animal falls dead to the ground. Alfred approaches the body and is further disappointed to discover it is just another a female. In a nearby bog, he finds her infant lying face down. He picks it up, and carries it home, bemused by the way that it plays with his beard hair.

I turn the page and keep reading, grimacing at the blatant cruelty of a man who is supposed to be one of the greatest naturalists to have ever lived. I am enraged at my parents for naming me after such a person. I wonder why so much knowledge from early natural history had to be gleaned from death. Jill would probably say that I am being too sensitive, like when, at age seven, I found a butterfly trapped inside a killing jar and set it free.

'That was a rare specimen!' she exclaimed.

'Then you shouldn't kill it!' I insisted, as Grandma Sue laughed heartily.

Jill was waiting for the black velvet creature to fall lifeless onto the ether soaked plaster-of-paris at the bottom of the jar so that she could pin it in her private collection. The ornate Lepidoptera were kept in a glass topped acacia box on her desk; specimens both arresting and ghoulish. Sometimes, I had nightmares about the butterflies' wings twitching to life, struggling against the slivers of metal that bound them, the whole board quivering until they freed themselves and folded upwards into the glass, liberated from death, but still sealed off from the world. I would wake gasping for air, driving my doughy fists upwards, as though I too lacked the strength to break through an invisible barrier. Once I realised that the air flowed freely around me, I still couldn't get back to sleep.

I feel no affinity with the gun-wielding conqueror in the book, but I am still drawn into the story. I want to know what made my father mark the passage. Back at his dwelling, Alfred can't find any milk for the baby orangutan, so he resolves instead to feed it a mixture of rice water and coconut milk. Over the following weeks, it moves onto a more solid diet of biscuit, eggs and sugar, but obviously malnourished, grows weaker and weaker. Trying to find a way to settle the creature, Alfred builds a makeshift mother out of buffalo skin, but the small animal only grows more agitated searching for a teat among the dead fur. However much he enjoys the company of his funny little orphan, the task of parenthood remains beyond him. Unsurprisingly, the animal eventually contracts a fever and dies.

I wonder if my father felt the same mixture of dread and delight that Alfred felt about the orangutan when he looked down at me as a baby. I wonder if he spent a lot of time sitting in this chair thinking about what it might have meant to be a father, about how hard it was for my mother to raise me. Contemplating all those years of feeding and placating me, I am filled with an intense gratitude towards Jill. It has been almost a month since we last spoke. Guilt gnaws at me.

'Can I have this?' I ask Oji.

He looks up from the drawer that he has now taken out of the desk so that he can sift through it more easily. 'Sure, sure, take whatever you want.'

His voice is agitated. With a huff, he picks up the drawer and empties the remaining items into the garbage bag with a load clash.

'Are you okay?'

'Yes, fine.'

Oji takes out the next drawer and without looking at what's inside, empties its contents into the bag, too. I put the book down and walk over to the desk.

'Hey,' I say soothingly. 'Do you want to take a break? Maybe have a cup of tea?'

Oji looks up, and I see that his face is streaked with tears.

'No,' he coughs. 'I just want this to be done.'

He takes out the third drawer unsteadily, and it slips from his grasp spilling papers all over the floor. 'Darn it!'

Oji kicks at the pile of paper, then leans against the wall.

'Hey,' I whisper. 'What is it? Come here.'

I take him by the arm and lead him to the armchair. He slumps down and tips his head back inhaling deeply. I sit on the coffee table unsure of what to do. Oji leans forward towards my father's half-finished bottle of whiskey and pours himself a shot. He drinks it in one gulp. Shaking his head and shoulders from the fiery rush, he purses his lips, then sits upright facing me.

'I'm sorry.'

'There's no need to be sorry. Just what's going on?'

Oji fidgets with his hands, not making eye contact. I'm worried. I don't know where this outburst has come from. He never drinks hard liquor. The pungent aroma of scotch hangs between us. I search the room for clues. The framed sketch of a kookaburra perched on a eucalypt branch looks at me with a mischievous expression.

'It's just… well… it's just that this is where it happened.'

I look back at Oji, unsure of what he means. 'Where what happened?'

Oji inhales again, then leans forward resting his chin on his hands. When he speaks his words are slow, as though it is taking all of his energy to keep his voice steady. 'Wallace,' he leans closer and touches my leg, 'I haven't been completely honest with you. Your father… it wasn't an accident. This is where he took his own life.'

I see Oji's lips moving but the words don't make sense. How can that be? I shake my head, my heart thudding in my chest. I slept in this room. On this floor. Looking at this bookcase, this chair. Is that why Oji was so uneasy about me setting up the air mattress in here when Jill came to stay? Suddenly, I feel like I might be sick.

'I haven't really been able to spend any time in here because… well, because this is where I found him. I should have told you earlier. Oh, goodness, I should have…'

'What? How?'

'Well, he was behind the desk over there.' Oji's voice cracks, but he continues. 'When I came in, there was this intense smell in the room. I had been on the mainland doing some errands, picking up his medication. I thought he was asleep, but then I saw the canister of nitrogen. At first, I was so confused.'

I keep shaking my head as though Oji's words might not be able to enter my ears, and then they might not be real. He takes both of his hands and holds my face still. Our eyes meet, and I see sadness so profound that I know he must be telling the truth.

Oji explains that my father found a man in Canberra who sells euthanisation equipment over the Internet. He still doesn't know how my father got the canister into the house without him seeing it, but he supposes that's why he asked him to go on the ferry on that particular day. He must have known that it was coming. Terry the postman must have delivered it right to the front door.

Was he afraid of dying? Did he have any second thoughts? Did he think about me at all on that final day? Maybe he read the passage about the orangutan that very morning.

'He didn't leave a note,' Oji is almost whispering now, but we are close enough that I can hear him clearly. 'I think that part hurt the most. Although I don't know what I would have wanted him to say. He was so sick, Wallace. He was going anyway, but I was still holding on.' I look down at Oji's hand gripping mine. 'I was still holding on, so tight. I would have gone on like that, caring for him, for years if he'd wanted.'

I picture my father in his last days, Oji looking after him the way that a mother looks after a child, but his task is that much more difficult because there is no future in it. My father is wearing flannel pyjamas, and he hasn't shaved in days. His skin is sallow, and his teeth are grey. He doesn't want to eat, no matter what Oji puts in front of him, even when Oji tries to coax him with Okonomiyaki and gyoza; he refuses, says everything tastes like cardboard.

I see him give a mournful grimace, saying something like 'I'm sorry you're stuck with this bag of bones.' Oji just laughs and replies, 'I wouldn't have it any other way.' Then I see Oji nestling himself under my father's shoulder, helping him to his feet, steering him to the bathroom, gently undoing the buttons on his pyjama shirt, then relieving him of his trousers. I see my father's wrinkled, naked, body inching down into a steaming hot bath, his sunken cheeks turning rosy.

Oji sits on the edge of the tub and bathes him with a wet cloth. They talk and talk, about anything and everything: what my father is reading in the *Kojiki*, the state of the world, the people back home who are finally retiring. I see them lying in bed, side by side, my father writhing in the restless sleep of the sick, while Oji listens to his breath.

In my vision, the skinny bird takes the place of my father and opens its eyes. I feel the weight of its head on my lap again, but when I look down it is just Oji's hand. All of my logic tries to convince me otherwise, but I can't help thinking that, maybe when my father left his body, he leapt sideways into another frail vessel.

Oji is speaking again. 'But of course he didn't want to go on like that. He didn't want to prolong it anymore. Who would want that? I suppose I was being selfish.'

My voice is cracking too. 'No, you're not selfish. You loved him.'

Oji cries on quietly. His sobs like asthmatic wheezes. His sweaty palm slips inside mine. I wrap my other arm around his shoulder.

'You don't know how many times I have thought about writing to that man who sold him the canister. Some days my letters are filled with rage, and then others I know that I should thank him, for letting him have that power over his own fate. Some days, I want to buy one for myself.'

'Don't say that.'

'Wallace, I'm so sorry.'

'Stop saying sorry.'

In the artificial darkness of the room, it feels like we are cocooned in this sadness. I can see out the door, but there is only a white wall; it is hard to believe that a day is in progress, that soon we will walk outside, and life will, one way or another, keep going.

'I was so eager for you to come because you're the only part of him that's left. And every day when you first arrived, I looked at you, and I saw him. It was the most incredible comfort. Now, I still see him, but I see you too, and I am just so disappointed that he never got to know you himself.'

Oji's tears are wet on my shoulder, mingling with mine.

'I've liked being here,' I say. 'It's helped me, too, you know?'

'It's why I had to renovate the house,' Oji wipes at his face. 'There was no way I could go on living here after I found him. But, even though he was sick, we were happy here. Some days in the beginning when we first arrived, he had these fits of energy, and we would forget. We would take a picnic into the bush, or play chess, and I could imagine another whole lifetime. We'd daydream about doing the place up... so I couldn't leave either. I had to create something new. The home that we dreamed about.'

I nod, everything making so much more sense. I feel so stupid for not figuring any of this out before. But there is still the curlew... the shape of it, the weight of it, the way that it speaks to me with its beak, its eyes.

'I suppose you think I'm crazy, then, for thinking he became a bird?'

Oji's face crinkles in sympathy. 'No, Wallace, I don't think you're crazy at all.'

'It's just that… well, when I saw the curlew, it was like I knew right away, that somehow it was him. Then, when you told me about the *Kojiki*, I thought you were giving me a clue.'

'I'm sorry, Wallace,' Oji looks down at the floor. 'When you started talking about all that business with the bird, I wanted so badly to believe you. I should have told you the truth but, after you came here, you never asked me any questions, and I was relieved. I didn't want to have to relive it. I was glad that, like me, you just seemed to want to push on.'

I let go of Oji's hand and pour some scotch into the second crystal glass. Oji pushes his glass forward for a refill. We empty the amber liquid in silence.

'I still think it's him,' I say.

Oji looks at me for a long time, searching my eyes.

'I can't explain it,' I lick the last of the scotch from my lips. 'But I saw him again, outside during the exhibition, and it was still like he was communicating with me.'

Oji looks down, not saying anything. He shakes his head.

'Wallace, it's just not…'

'Would you like to see for yourself?'

Oji takes a handkerchief out of his pocket, wipes at his nose, and then blows loudly. His skin is blotched. He looks much older under the overhead bulb.

'Yes,' he sighs. 'Yes, I really would.'

I sniffle and smooth the tender skin under my eyes. 'Okay. Good.'

I refill our glasses again squeezing my eyes shut as I tip my head back and drink.

Common trees: bangalow palm, blueberry ash, broad leaf paperbark, brush box, coastal banksia, eprapah wattle, forest she-oak, grey myrtle, macaranga, native frangipani…

Pain shoots up my shins as I follow Peter down the Whistling Kite Trail. It feels like we have been walking for miles.

Native mulberry, pink euodia, pink tip bottlebrush, plunkett mallee, scribbly gum, small leafed lilly-pilly, tallowwood, water gum, wheel of fire… I look back down at Peter's book listing the names of the local plants with pictures and descriptions. I wonder who named them. Was it some plump, old, white man like Alfred Russel Wallace? I'd much prefer to know the native names, but I don't tell Peter that. I know that he is just trying to be nice, and I appreciate him coming to visit me, even though the bird work is mostly done.

'Just a waiting game now,' he told me on the drive to the trail. 'Once they all set off, we'll start getting weekly reports back. Something like the co-ordinates I showed you last time, but this time, they'll be spread all over the globe. Or running along that specific migratory bird highway, to be more exact. The East-Asian Australasian Flyway, they call it.'

He pronounces the name like he is reading for a documentary.

When we reach a clearing with a large fallen trunk in the centre, I stop to catch my breath. 'Mind if we sit for a minute?'

'Sounds good to me.'

Peter plonks himself down on the log next to me, and I look up at the ring of towering eucalypts surrounding us, a halo of sunshine falling over the dried leaves at our feet. A skink scurries through the leaves then stops suddenly, the shiny membrane of its back changing colour as it flicks its tail from side to side. I unzip my bag and take out my water bottle, gulping a mouthful. I hold the bottle up to Peter, but he shakes his head and takes out his own.

'So, heading off soon then, are you?

I nod my head.

After the exhibition, I decided that it was time to start thinking about going back to Sydney. I received an email from the university that said I'd been accepted for the Masters program. I still don't know if it's what I want to do, but I suppose that I might as well try. Sarah was excited to hear the news, or as excited as someone can be in a long stream of text messages. There were a lot of smiley faces. I am nervous to see Sarah again, but I think the time away has helped. It's allowed me to miss her and decide what about our friendship is most important to me.

I haven't told Jill yet.

'Next week.' I feel a sudden sense of panic saying it out loud.

Detecting my discomfort, Peter gives me a reassuring nod. 'Good girl. You'll be right.'

'Thank you,' I say. 'For everything.'

Peter smiles, picks up a stick off the ground and inspects its bark closely.

'Nothing to thank me for.'

He doesn't make eye contact, just twirls the stick between his fingers. I know that it might be a long time before I see Peter again, so I push on through his bashfulness.

'No, really. I appreciate all the time you've put into teaching me about the curlews, coming out here to see Oji and me. It means a lot.'

Peter shrugs his shoulders. 'I come because I want to. You aren't bad company, you two.' He opens his mouth as if he is trying to articulate some deeper emotion, but instead just laughs and takes another sip of his water. 'I've never been much good with words.'

I stretch my legs out straight, lean back on my arms, and turn my face up towards the sun. 'Don't worry; me neither.'

I can hear Peter's boots push through the foliage as he reclines himself, too.

I will miss the steady song of the bush. The way that the twittering birds are layered one on top of the other and the slightest change in the wind shifts the octave of the leaves. There is something that I have wanted to ask Peter, and I know that I am running out of time, so I open my eyes and turn towards him.

'Hey...' I break our silence. 'I was wondering if you might want to try something with me?'

Peter looks at me, intrigued. 'Well, that depends what it is. I did all my experimenting with drugs back in the seventies.'

I laugh loudly. 'Nothing like that.'

Peter looks pleased with himself at having made me smile. 'Well, what then?'

'Remember how you said that my father was doing the bird calls?'

'Yeah?'

'Well... do you think we could give it a try?'

Peter laughs for a moment, then leans over his knees clasping his hands together. 'I don't know. I wouldn't know where to start.'

'Me neither, but...'

I can't explain to Peter that I haven't finished what I came here to do. While I didn't arrive on the island with a particular mission, I have felt the whole time that some predetermined path was laid out for me. By my father? I don't know. But now that I have decided to leave, I am worried that I won't reach the end, and so many questions will remain unanswered. Unsure of where the urge comes from, I place my hands on my waist and press down with the tips of my fingers. Subtle vibrations pulsate through my skin.

Peter watches, bemused. 'Just as odd as your old man.' The gusty wind continues as gum nuts and small branches fall from the trees. 'But I mean that as a compliment.'

I grin and press my fingers harder. 'Try this.'

Peter narrows his eyes and shakes his head as if to say, 'I don't know,' but puts his water bottle down on the ground and follows my lead.

His stocky fingers press into his beige polo shirt, thick blue veins on the back of his hands bulging. The vibrations under my own fingertips increase in intensity.

'Can you feel that?'

Peter raises his eyebrows. 'Hah, actually, I can.'

He massages his waist and starts to wriggle his shoulders.

Pressing my fingers closer, I feel like a lever is pressed; my head tilts back so that I am looking up at the circle of blue sky. A long oboe-like note discharges from my throat.

'Not bad,' Peter laughs, and then presses his fingers down harder too.

His sound is a shorter warble that echoes around the clearing with mine. Continuing to push, I can feel the cries forming, a percussive rhythm, like a heartbeat that pulses through my whole body. It is a pleasant sensation. Watching Peter, I see his bare arms come up in goose bumps as he rocks his head back again.

Our looping cries ascend.

Yesterday, when I told Oji that I'd be leaving next week because I'd got into the Masters, he looked down at his crossword puzzle and nodded his head.

Scribbling in the boxes, he cleared his throat. 'Yes, yes of course. You should go. It sounds like a good course. You will come to visit though, won't you?'

I stood up and wrapped my arms around his shoulders, 'Of course. I didn't put all this work into renovating just so you can live like a king.'

I didn't want to think about how much I was going to miss Oji, so I busied myself cleaning the kitchen; spraying water at a long stream of ants that had decided to make themselves at home in the breadbasket.

Today, I am coming to terms with all the people I have to say goodbye to. I know I will return, but I don't know what will change between now and then. Making my way to the house from the IGA, the ingredients for Okonomiyaki swing at my side in a plastic bag. I am determined to show Oji that I have mastered his recipe. On my way, in the memorial park, I am glad to see Milly sitting by the monument. She has her back to me and is talking to her mother again. I don't want to startle her, so I announce my arrival.

'Hi,' I shout.

Seeing me, Milly jumps to her feet and comes bounding at me like an excited puppy. She is wearing a bright pink tracksuit. As she hugs me, she knocks the groceries out of my hand.

'Hey, how are you? I like your outfit.'

She looks up at me with a gappy grin. 'My aunty Linda gave it to me.'

'Oh,' I say. 'How pretty.'

I am relieved to hear that there's another adult in Milly's life, maybe someone that can look out for her. 'Do you like Aunty Linda?'

Milly nods. 'She looks a bit like Mum, and she doesn't let Dad yell at me.'

'That's good. Your dad isn't around now, is he?'

Milly shakes her head vehemently. 'No. My dad is a dickhead.'

I open my mouth in surprise. 'Where did you learn a word like that?'

Milly trills, still holding onto me. 'Aunty Linda says it all the time!'

I think about telling her that she shouldn't swear but stop myself. She'll probably need a few swear words in her artillery. Unwrapping her arms from my legs, I pick up the plastic bag, and we walk back hand in hand towards the circular garden.

'I haven't seen you in ages, Wallace. My dad said you'd probably gone back to wherever you came from.'

I look down at her expectant eyes. 'I *came* from Sydney.'

'I don't care where you came from. Because you're my friend. Did you know you look just like the yellow Power Ranger?'

I don't tell Milly that I am pretty sure the yellow Power Ranger is Vietnamese. It isn't the first time I've heard the comparison. The show was popular when I was her age. I suppose they must still be playing re-runs on TV. When we reach her mother's memorial stone, I crouch down in front of Milly.

'I was hoping to see you to say goodbye. I'm going to be leaving soon.'

Milly sticks out her bottom lip in an exaggerated pout and shakes her head.

'But I was thinking, if you want, we can be pen-pals?'

Milly's expression changes and she nods enthusiastically. 'Yessss! I can send you pictures, and you can tell me all the secrets about your boyfriends.'

'I don't have any boyfriends,' I laugh, 'but you can tell me whatever you want.'

I reach into the plastic bag and pull out a box of stamps that I bought at the post office.

'This is important,' I place the box in Milly's small hands. 'These are stamps. So, every time you want to send me a letter, you just put one of these on the envelope with my address. I am sure if you need help, the very nice ladies at the post office will do it for you.'

I recall Megan Riley's confession at the RSL, and am not sure how nice she is, but am hopeful her discrimination doesn't extend to little girls.

Milly looks at the pictures of Australian wildflowers on the box.

'They aren't stickers,' I add. 'You can only use them on the envelopes you send to me, okay? One at a time.'

Milly agrees and wraps her arms around my neck. I hug her back.

'Don't show these to your dad,' I whisper. 'Hide them somewhere good.'

Letting go, Milly nods again and sits down on the ground, inspecting the box closely. I stand and walk around the monument, reading the plaques as I go. On the adjacent side to the plaque for Milly's mother, I see it.

AKI MATSUMOTO

18TH AUGUST 1954 – 7TH SEPTEMBER 2017

The dark plate is affixed to a square of sand-coloured concrete and is embossed with gold letters. It is identical in size and format to all the others.

A few weeks ago, I asked Oji if my father's ashes were in the garden.

'I never go there,' he told me. 'To me, your father will never be concealed beneath a stone.'

For me, either. One way or another, I know that he needed to ascend.

When I broached the subject, we were sitting at the kitchen table, sipping tea, still emotionally exhausted from the conversation in the study.

'Why did you pay for it then?' I asked.

Oji shrugged. 'Kate told me that, one day, I might want the reminder. A place to go and remember him. I couldn't argue. She helped me organise everything. Plus, to be honest, I didn't really want an urn around the house. It felt, too, depressing? Morbid?'

'Sure, that makes sense.'

Now, standing over my father's name, I look down at the neat letters, trying to conjure a response.

'You can talk to him if you want,' Milly peeps from behind me.

I ruffle her hair. 'I have been talking to him, just not here.'

She scrunches up her nose. 'That's weird.'

I laugh. 'Yeah, maybe it is.'

Giving Milly one last hug, I tuck a piece of paper with my Sydney address inside her tracksuit pocket.

'If you ever lose it, just ask Oji.'

Milly's eyes are glassy, but she holds back her tears and gives a stern nod, like she has had plenty of practice with goodbyes.

I start to walk back cross the park towards the footpath. 'You're a tough cookie. I'll miss you.'

'I'll miss you, too, Wallace.'

When I look back over my shoulder, Milly is pirouetting in circles, her red hair fanning out. Faster and faster, she turns, until she topples down on the grass.

I picture walking by her on a Sydney street, years from now. Hair ironed straight as a sheet of copper, angular hips jutting through her jeans; she carries herself with a modelish confidence. Every person she passes, she looks straight in the eye. Somehow, I recognise her immediately, but her eyes brush over my face. She has forgotten me entirely. This whole island and all of its inhabitants are nothing but a distant, spinning memory.

12

Moths crash into the light bulb next to the front door. The dusty figures jostle, casting magnified shadows over the wooden deck.

The phone rings in my ear. Once. Twice. Three times. Four. I wait hopefully for my mother's message bank so that she will have to call me back, and I will have the option of avoiding her calls for a while longer. I do want to speak to her, but I don't know exactly what I want to say. My anger towards Jill is muddled with all the other confusing things I have been feeling. I know that I am holding her responsible for much more than she deserves.

After the fifth ring, Jill answers, a little breathless.

'Hello? Wallace?'

'Hi,' I murmur.

'Thank god! I've been trying to get a hold of you for weeks…'

I fidget, leaning against the railing. 'I know. I'm…'

'I'm sor…'

'You go.'

'You go.'

We both laugh and speak at the same time. 'I'm sorry.'

At the sound of my mother's voice, I relax. I don't have to say anything; she has already put our fight behind her in that selfless way that mothers do.

'What are you doing? You sound puffed.'

'I was gardening, actually.'

I'm confused; Jill doesn't have a garden. She lives on the top floor of her building and her balcony is completely paved.

'I set up an herb garden,' her voice is proud.

I imagine her planting seedlings in terracotta boxes overlooking the harbour, as the Manly ferry cuts its way under the bridge. I am glad that she is finally using the floral gardening gloves and pink handled tools that she bought years ago when she decided that she wanted to grow tomatoes. Back then, I laughed at how even getting dirty was an exercise in fashion. The tomatoes died within a fortnight, but I don't remind Jill about the shriveled brown balls, or the brittle stalks that went black in the sun.

'That's great.'

'It's very soothing, actually. You'll see it for yourself when you get home. Not that you have to… Just when…'

I cut her off. 'I am coming home. Actually, that's why I'm calling.'

Jill sighs deeply. 'Oh, Wallace, that's such good news.'

I can tell that she has a long list of questions that she wants to ask but doesn't want to upset me again.

'I got into the Masters program.'

She gives a little shriek. 'That's, well, fabulous. If that's what you want to do?'

The phone line crackles a little; I lean out over the balcony to get a clearer signal. It's early evening and the street is cast in dimmer colours.

'Yeah, I think so. I mean, I don't know. But we'll see.'

'I'm sure you're going to love it.'

I can hear Jill moving around her apartment, organising the magazines on the coffee table. There is a clinking of plates, as though she might be emptying the dishwasher. It is going to be strange to immerse in the domestic habits of my mother again. A towel draped over the dining chair each morning, the scent of her laundry powder, so different from Oji's.

'Wallace, I do want to say that I'm sorry that I never talked to you more, about your father and me.'

I interrupt. 'It's okay, I understand.'

There is the distant sound of liquid pouring into a glass, and I know she must be drinking wine.

She swallows. 'It's not okay. It's just, well, he really hurt me. And I didn't want him to do the same to you. I thought I was protecting you. Just know that I always wanted the best for you. Truly.'

'I forgive you.' A weight lifts from my chest. 'But I am going to start learning Japanese again.'

I tell my mother that I found an evening course in the city, and that I've already enrolled.

'That's good, Wallace. Really. I should never have discouraged you… I just…'

'It's okay. But will you practice with me?'

'Sure, but I was never very good at it myself. Your father wasn't a very patient teacher.'

I watch lights start to flick on inside the neighbouring houses as I absorb my mother's words. Silhouettes move behind the drapes, and I wonder what routines make a home? What aggregate of tasks and chores and daily movements culminate in a family? I think about how vulnerable my mother must have been when my father left. To be in love with a man whom she knew could never truly love her back – a child on the way. To be trying to learn a new language just to communicate with him better – to try and close the distance between them. But the distance was nothing to do with language. It must have been so difficult for her to have to move back to live with her mother when what she really wanted was to start a family of her own. But, all my life, I never sensed her fear or anger at all. She hid it so well. Maybe too well, because I never gave her the credit she deserved.

'Thank you,' I say.

'For what?'

'For everything.'

Jill lets out a sound somewhere between a cough and a laugh. 'You're welcome. What's gotten into you? You sound different, you know?'

'I don't know. Good different or bad different?'

'Just different.'

'I feel different.'

I turn away from the street to face the house again. I can see Oji in the kitchen reaching for something on the upper shelf of the pantry. Jill keeps talking in my ear. She is saying something about the latest couple getting married on TV, giddy with excitement. Her words flutter like the moth shadows moving across the ground.

'So, the audition is next month.'

'Wait, what audition?'

'Haven't you been listening? I can't believe they're actually interested in me.'

I realise that Jill isn't just talking about the show; she is talking about being on the show. I laugh and am filled with pride. Jill deserves happiness, and, while I doubt that this is going to lead her to Mr. Right, I am impressed that she is willing to give it a try. I wonder what the people in her office will say but know that she wouldn't care either way. I'm sure that she loves people talking about her behind her back, and not even out of narcissism. I think she genuinely likes to entertain.

'Of course they're interested in you.'

'Will you come with me? To the studio.'

'Sure, I'd love to.'

'No sarcasm? No snide remarks?'

I laugh. 'No, can't I just be happy for you?'

I can see it now. My mother and I walking to the glitzy TV studio just around the corner from her house, stopping at the café that she likes – the one she has been going to for over a decade where the old Italian couple know her name. Mrs. Cerretto asks how my studies are going, and I say the same thing that I have said since I was in high school, 'studying hard,' to which she beams, 'good girl,' and gives my mother a congratulatory wink.

We enter through the big electric doors of the studio. Jill is wearing the tight red dress she always wears when she needs a little extra confidence, hair perfectly blow-dried, make-up a little too heavy. A young hotshot producer in an expensive suit greets us, paying Jill a barrage of compliments that almost sound sincere. I hover in the background, texting Sarah about all the C-grade celebrities walking around.

For the first time, I feel excited about the prospect of going home. Or, at least, going back to that version of home. Because hasn't this become home, too? I wonder how different I really am and while there is no exact measurement for how a person changes over time, am sure that the accumulation of shifts inside me might constitute another person, worthy of another home. Oji and I stripped out the old and unwanted parts of the house, and replaced them with new ones – and unwittingly, maybe I have created a new identity here.

While I still can't reconcile myself with my father's Japanese heritage, I have started to feel like my body contains an important history of its own. One that started with a broken relationship between my parents, two stories running parallel, bought together again on this island, by a kind old man who has taught me more than I ever expected to learn.

Inside, Oji has his back to me stirring something in a saucepan, steam curling around him. I listen to him humming along to the jazz playing in the background, and feel like I am looking into the future, at his life without me. A meal for one. Conversationless rooms. The breeze chills my arms. I want to go back inside. If the me that is here right now is different to the one that left Sydney, I wish that we could both exist. Like those versions that proliferate in the process of grieving. Maybe I can leave a copy to live with Oji, while I also go back to Sydney to start a new chapter.

Sensing my eyes on him, Oji turns and gives me a wave. I wave back, catching my own reflection in the glass.

Jill keeps talking, but I am distracted – poised on the edge of two worlds.

Honk, honk, honk.

The sound of an unfamiliar horn blaring outside rouses me from the couch. I'm not expecting Peter today, and I've become accustomed to his ute's long beeps. Maybe the Wrights have a visitor, or maybe Ben got a new car and is tooting to hurry his mother. I look out the window and see Diego behind the wheel of a bright teal Kombi van, chrome trim shining. He climbs down from the cabin and waves me outside.

'What are you doing?' I shout from the front steps.

'I traded in the Commodore.'

I open my mouth in disbelief. 'Oh, my god, you're having a mid-life crisis, aren't you?'

Diego throws his head back and scoffs. 'Fuck off. I'm not that old.'

'Well, unless you plan to live past 80, you kind of are…'

He rolls his eyes as I walk around the van, inspecting the glossy paint, peering in the side windows at the double mattress and wooden drawers for storing cooking equipment, or whatever it is that campers take on the road with them. Diego's guitar is strapped into a rack behind the driver's seat.

'Wanna go for a drive?'

I eye him suspiciously. 'Is this really yours?'

'Yes! What do you think? I stole it?' He gets back in. 'Come on!'

'Ok…' The bench seats are cream vinyl; the steering wheel made of polished wood, inset with pearly flecks. 'This must have cost you a fortune.'

Diego shrugs. 'I don't have anything better to spend my money on. I've got to cut back on the beers anyway.'

He turns the ignition, and the engine gives a vintage cough as he shifts the gear stick mounted behind the steering wheel. We cruise towards the jetty.

'Try the stereo,' Diego beams. 'It's the one thing that isn't original.'

I twist the volume knob and a sonic boom bursts from the speakers reverberating around the car, rattling the pine drawers in the back. It's some INXS song that I can't remember the name of. Diego thrashes his head back and forth, his hair falling over his eyes.

'Careful!'

'You're one to be giving me driving tips.'

In the car park near the ferry terminal, Diego parks the van, and we sit looking out over the water as office workers board towards the mainland for another dull day tucked inside city towers.

'So,' Diego says turning to me, 'I was wondering if you might want some company on the drive back to Sydney?'

I give him a sideways look. 'I'm not driving...'

'But you could be,' he urges. 'We could take this old girl on an adventure.'

I stare at him to see if he is serious. 'Really?'

'Yes, really! Why the mood today?'

'I don't know, you're acting weird.'

Diego turns away from me and looks out through the windscreen at a whistling kite drawing wide circles with its rigid wings. I trace its hovering trajectory too.

'Why do you want to go to Sydney?'

'Well, there's someone there I want to see.'

I remember the woman he mentioned when he told me about coming to Australia. 'Your old girlfriend?'

He sighs. 'Yes and no. There was one part I didn't tell you.'

Diego avoids my gaze. 'Mmm?'

His attention shifts, and I notice that the shell I gave him for Christmas is stuck to the dashboard with a piece of blu-tac, the peach rim of its opening pointing forwards. He stares at the small object intently, and I am touched to see that he kept it.

'I have a daughter.'

When I turn my head sharply towards him, he meets my eye.

'Don't give me that look.'

'There's no look. I'm just… surprised.'

I absorb Diego's words as stragglers in suits run to catch their boat. The last is a man who is wearing rubber sandals with business socks, his leather dress shoes in hand. Diego is still staring at the shell, as though the sentence he wants might come creeping out of it like a hermit crab.

'Yeah, well, I haven't seen her since she was a baby. She'd be, god, almost eleven now.'

'Right,' I nod.

I am not exactly surprised that Diego didn't share this news with me. I suppose he felt sorry for me because of my father and didn't want to dredge up any old emotions on top of what I was already dealing with. Or maybe he thought that I'd be angry with him for replicating the typical story of a man abandoning his family. I wonder if that's part of why he didn't want to touch me. He couldn't see past the daughter in me, and I awoke the father in him.

'So, why now? Why go back?'

'Well,' he leans forward and unsticks the shell, turning it over in his hand, 'I don't know. Maybe it's spending all this time with you. Thinking about what your old man missed out on.'

I lean my back against the window and turn to face Diego, one leg curling under me on the bench seat the other stretching forward. 'And what if she doesn't want to see you?'

'Well, I guess I'll find out. But I've got to try.'

Diego's face is tense. I think about how many times my father might have had the same inclination. What would I have done if he'd shown up on my doorstep? Would I have known it was him right away? Or would I have gone shy like I always did when a salesman came to the door, shouting down the hallway for Jill or Grandma Sue. For a moment, I am angry with my

177

mother again. I imagine her turning him away, holding me back behind her as she closes the door in his face. Then, I remind myself that it isn't my mother's fault. He could have come. If he wanted to badly enough, he would have.

I nod. 'Yeah, I suppose you do.'

'So, I thought we could drive together, seeing as you're going anyway. You could get some practice in. We could stop for a surf on the coast.'

My expression brightens. 'You surf?'

'Not well, but I recall you telling me that you're pretty rusty, too. My mate has some boards he can lend us. We can throw them in the back.'

I eye the mattress in the back nervously, and, as though reading my mind, Diego interjects. 'I have a tent, too. You can have the bed.'

I smile. 'Ok,' I murmur cautiously.

'Yeah?'

I give a tentative nod, and Diego cheers. He holds his hand up for a high five and I slap it with mine. The energy inside the van lifts, and I am staring down a long stretch of road with Diego at the wheel. There we are, cruising past the Gold Coast, pulling in at Byron Bay, paddling out into the slow peeling waves, laughing as we tumble into the water next to children on foam boards. Then passing Grafton, Coffs Harbour, Newcastle. A thousand kilometres of paddocks, mountains, road works, single pub towns. Cheap coffee. Dry spinach and ricotta rolls from the service station. A tent pitched in the dying light. A thousand kilometres of him and me. Music. Conversation. Silence.

'So, what's your daughter's name?'

'Victoria. We named her after my grandmother.'

'Why'd you leave?' I press.

'Look, there will be plenty of time for all that when we're on the road.' Diego flicks the ignition and turns up the music. 'But, for now, it's time to rock!'

I cringe, 'No. No. No. I'm definitely going to be DJ.'

Diego pretends he can't hear me and turns the knob further to the right. I try to push his hand away, but he bats me off with his other hand. We laugh as the bass thrums. and I give in, resting my head against the window.

'This is going to be fun,' Diego smirks as he drums along on the dash with two fingers.

'Oji!'

I call from the back deck.

The Morning Glory buds that were closed yesterday have blossomed. The planter box is filled with deep blue flowers. Oji doesn't respond, so I go inside to look for him. On the dining table there is a cup of tea, hardly touched. A slimy beige film has started to form on its surface. Where is he?

'Oji?'

I walk down the hallway towards his bedroom, but find it empty too. He isn't anywhere in the house. Looking out the front window, I see that his car is still parked in the driveway. My heart beats a little faster. It isn't like Oji to go out without telling me and, even less, to go out on foot. I survey the kitchen bench and the refrigerator but there is no note, no sign of where he might be.

Just to be certain that he didn't slip by me while I was tending to the flowers, I go out back again and scan the yard. Nothing. Just a lone bush turkey meandering across the mowed lawn. From the edge of the balcony, I look down the side of the house, but there are only two white sheets on the clothesline billowing in the breeze.

I replay the conversation that we had over breakfast; Oji didn't mention anything about his plans for the day. He didn't say much at all actually, just filled in his crossword while I completed the online enrolment for my classes. 70146 Art and

Curatorship, 70155 Managing Collections, 70162 Engaging Audiences. After selecting my core subjects, I couldn't decide which elective to take for the semester. I was leaning towards 70144 Death and Disease in Renaissance Art, although I supposed that 70168 The Business of Art might be more useful in acquiring a job.

'What do you think?' I asked Oji.

He looked up. 'I think you should do whatever makes you happy.'

'You're right,' I smiled, selecting my first preference, and reading over the course outline.

Skimming over the contents of the unit, I couldn't wait to learn about the interplay between art and disease – and what they called the prophylactic role of images. I started to feel like I was making the right decision after all – that maybe, just like Oji said, I just need to do the things that make me happy, and not worry so much. It doesn't matter that maybe my choices aren't the most practical. My father travelled the world as a young scientist, chasing birds, darting between jobs. And Oji followed his heart out of his marriage, into a life with my father, all the way to another country. I don't think I ever saw Grandma Sue make a practical decision – she was always led by what the waves were doing on any given day – and she still acquired enough to leave an inheritance for her family. I suppose my mother is the most practical person in my life, and even she is trying to be on reality TV.

In the kitchen, I notice that the unwashed breakfast bowls are still in the sink, breadcrumbs scattered around the base of the toaster. Oji never leaves the house without doing the dishes, which only intensifies my concern. I grab his car keys from the hook and decide to go looking for him. First, I try the IGA, but he isn't there, or in the café either. Kate says she hasn't seen him.

'I am sure he's just popped over to one of the neighbors' places. You know Oji, loves a chat.'

I nod but am sure that isn't the case.

Driving back along the road to the house, I remember what Oji said about wanting a canister for himself sometimes, and panic seizes me. My hands grip the steering wheel so hard that my knuckles turn white. Maybe the thought of being alone is too much now that I am leaving. He wouldn't, would he? But if he did, it would be like him to go somewhere else, to spare me the pain of finding him. Then, I remember what else we spoke about that day in the study. My unkept promise. I keep driving towards the far southern end of the island.

The car park at Sandy Beach is empty, beer cans strewn across the ground. Resting against one of the wooden posts, there is a plastic bottle made into a bong, a quarter full with inky water.

Today, the beach is murky and dormant under a cloudy sky. Barefoot, I walk down over the short stretch of white sand, onto the flats coated in green-brown slime. Dark worms of mud wriggle out between my toes. The cold ground sends a chill through my feet. Although Oji hasn't mentioned it to me again, I have a hunch that he has come here to see my father. Of course, he wants to meet the curlew that I have spoken so much about, but I haven't been able to bring myself back to the beach, because that will mean having to say goodbye myself.

In the distance, I hear a morose cry. It's low tide, so I follow the sound of the curlews to my usual counting spot. As I walk, I think about the curlew poems from my father's collection and wonder why we are so intent on projecting our sadness onto birds.

For Yeats, his curlews recalled passion-dimmed eyes. For Thomas, they were a spectre of dark womanly pain. For me, they sing every unnamable feeling that still turns in me whenever I think about my father. But I remind myself of the highlighted passage from a Lord Grey bird watching compendium. He says that the cry of the curlew is anything but sad. *The notes do not sound passionate: they suggest peace, rest, healing, joy, an assurance of happiness past, present and to come.* Nearing closer to the calls,

I try to hear the sounds as Lord Grey heard them, and maybe my father, too; calming like a meditation gong. Like the sound of the women chanting in Kate's den.

I see Oji standing, facing the birds. He is still dressed in his cotton pyjama shorts and a white t-shirt, his bare legs etched with a spidery network of purple veins. He is barefoot, too, and his feet are almost buried below the surface of the mud, as though he has been standing in the same place for a long time, and the ground is slowly absorbing him. Four or five metres in front of Oji, three curlews pierce the ground in search of food. As I get closer, he turns towards me but doesn't move.

'You found me.'

'I was worried.'

'I'm sorry. I just had to come.'

I nod and stand next to him, looking at the birds. My father stops pacing and turns towards us. I recognise him right away. Oji looks into the bird's eyes, and he opens and closes his mouth slowly a few times, as though he wants to say something, but no words come out. He looks at me, and then back at the curlew.

'Is that...?'

I don't really need to confirm anything. Oji's knowing has already confirmed itself in the same way as mine did.

The curlew takes three angular steps, bending at the knee, extending forward in jilted strides. Oji squats down so that he and my father are at the same level. There are no words or sounds exchanged between them, but they seem to be having a conversation with their eyes. I don't interrupt, but wait patiently, my hand resting on Oji's shoulder. After a while, the bird looks up at me.

'Hi,' I whisper. 'I hope you don't mind that I told him about you.'

My father pecks the ground twice.

'He says he doesn't mind.'

'I know he doesn't,' Oji smiles with tears in his eyes.

The other two curlews, still further away, turn their necks suddenly towards the sound of a car passing on the road just beyond the mangroves.

My father looks towards them, craning his neck from side to side as the sound fades, and then looks back at us. To me, he appears to be torn, but maybe he feels nothing about leaving. I have no way of knowing if there is any trace of human emotion left in his bird body, his bird mind.

I look away to hide my sadness. 'I suppose you're going then?'

He gives the ground a single peck.

I breathe in deeply. Oji stands and puts his arm around my waist, resting his head on my shoulder. My father turns from us, and with bounding steps, opens his wings. Sun cracks through the clouds, and streams of light fall over the tidal flats. Oji looks up towards the unexpected warmth, a bar of sunshine falling across his face. Tears glisten on his cheeks. He looks back towards my father, and we both watch on silently as he beats his wings forcefully, until he lifts off the ground.

'Aki,' Oji whispers.

A few gusty strokes propel my father up and forwards, then he settles into a smoother rhythm where only the tips of his wings are pulsating to keep him elevated. The shadows shift on the water below him, as though he is conducting the light with the variegated edges of his feathers.

He doesn't pause or turn back. Smaller, and smaller, and smaller he becomes.

And then, he is gone.

Epilogue

In the Art Gallery of New South Wales, a man wearing white gloves takes a heavy gilt frame down from the wall. He removes the plaque with a flat tool – *Jan Davidsz De Heem, Still life with flowers in a glass vase, 1665-70* – and places the sliver of metal in a pouch around his waist.

Loading the image into a slatted trolley, he carefully positions it to avoid the frame bumping against any of the other cargo. Wrapping the piece in a large protective cloth, he doesn't look at the reflection of the window in the vase, but, if he did, he'd see a flock of curlews flying, their long beaks pointing forwards like arrows.

Across the skyscape, beyond the visible framed vista, the birds flap their wings. Every part of their bodies aches. They have been flying for days and they are much fewer now than when they started. The whole world lay at their backs, while the whole world still stretches ahead. It is a grand and purposeful loop.

Before long, the influx of bodies will weigh on the axis of the earth and the balance will tip again, shooting them back down the other side towards the place from which they have come, and will return, again and again. For now, they mercifully inch towards rest.

The land below takes shape, and some internal pull signals that this is the final stop. One by one, the curlews peel off and glide down towards the flats. Nearing the ground, they pierce a living atmosphere, the air effervescent with insects. Beneath their feet, the ground is wet; larvae spring forth from the melted frost.

They only have to open their beaks to get their fill.

The feast – it lasts for days.

References

Britten, Benjamin. *Curlew River: A Parable for Church Performance, Op. 71*. London: Faber Music, 1964.

Hāmana, Hēnare. Te Karanga a Te Huia: The Call of the Huia. Radio interview, 2YA, 1949. Accessed February 1, 2020. Ngā Taonga Sound & Vision.

Grey, Lord. *The Charm of the Birds*. London: Faber and Faber, 1927.

Oliveros, Pauline. *Sonic Meditations*. Baltimore: Smith Publications, 1974.

Ō no Yasumaro. *The Kojiki: Records of Ancient Matters*. Translated by Basil Hall Chamberlain. Tokyo: Asiatic Society of Japan, 1882.

Thomas, Dylan. "In the White Giant's Thigh". In *Collected Poems: 1934–1952*, 178-180. New York: New Directions, 1953.

Wallace, Alfred Russel. *The Malay Archipelago: The Land of the Orang-Utan, and the Bird of Paradise*. London: Macmillan, 1869.

Yeats, W. B. "He Reproves the Curlew". In *The Wind Among the Reeds*, 58. London: Elkin Mathews, 1899.

www.ingramcontent.com/pod-product-compliance
Lightning Source LLC
Chambersburg PA
CBHW051834020726
47502CB00005B/1787